TELL THEM OF BATTLES,
KINGS, AND ELEPHANTS

TELL THEM OF BATTLES, KINGS & ELEPHANTS

Mathias Énard

Translated by Charlotte Mandell

A NEW DIRECTIONS BOOK

Originally published in French as *Parle-leur de batailles, de rois et d'éléphants* by Actes Sud in 2010
Published by arrangement with the French Publishers' Agency

The drawing by Michelangelo on p. 6 is from the Archivio Buonarroti, copyright © 2018 Associazione MetaMorfosi, Rome.
The drawing on pp. 134–135 is by Pierre Marquès, copyright © Pierre Marquès.

Manufactured in the United States of America
New Directions Books are printed on acid-free paper
First published clothbound by New Directions in 2018

Library of Congress Cataloging-in-Publication Data
Names: Énard, Mathias, 1972– author. | Mandell, Charlotte, translator.
Title: Tell them of battles, kings, and elephants / Mathias Enard ; translated by Charlotte Mandell.
Other titles: Parle-leur de batailles, de rois et d'elephants. English
Description: New York : New Directions, 2018.
Identifiers: LCCN 2018021250 (print) | LCCN 2018026918 (ebook) |
ISBN 9780811227056 (ebook) | ISBN 9780811227049 (alk. paper)
Subjects: LCSH: Michelangelo Buonarroti, 1475–1564—Fiction. | Bridges—Fiction. | Golden Horn (Turkey)—Fiction. | Istanbul (Turkey)—Fiction. |
GSAFD: Biographical fiction. | Historical fiction.
Classification: LCC PQ2705.N273 (ebook) | LCC PQ2705.N273 P3713 2018 (print) |
DDC 843/.92—dc23
LC record available at https://lccn.loc.gov/2018021250

10 9 8 7 6 5 4 3 2 1

New Directions Books are published for James Laughlin
by New Directions Publishing Corporation
80 Eighth Avenue, New York 10011

Tell them of what thou alone hast seen, then what thou hast heard, and since they be children tell them of battles and kings, horses, devils, elephants, and angels, but omit not to tell them of love and suchlike.

pani dua
ù bochal dui no
una ariga
tortegli

una salata
e quatro pani
ù bochal di dolco
ò un ucciero di brusciò
ù piattello di spinaci
quatro alici
tortelli

sei pani
dua minestre di finochio
una aringa
ù bochal di tondo

NIGHT DOES NOT COMMUNICATE WITH THE DAY. IT burns up in it. Night is carried to the stake at dawn. And its people along with it—the drinkers, the poets, the lovers. We are a people of the banished, of the condemned. I do not know you. I know your Turkish friend; he is one of ours. Little by little he is vanishing from the world, swallowed up by the shadows and their mirages; we are brothers. I don't know what pain or what pleasure propelled him to us, to stardust, maybe opium, maybe wine, maybe love; maybe some obscure wound of the soul deep-hidden in the folds of memory.

You want to join us.

Your fear and confusion propel you into our arms; you want to nestle in there, but your tough body keeps clinging to its certainties; it pushes desire away, refuses to surrender.

I don't blame you.

You live in another prison, a world of strength and bravery where you think you can be carried aloft in triumph; you think you can win the goodwill of the powerful, you seek glory and wealth. But when night falls, you tremble. You don't drink, for you are afraid; you know that the burning sensation of alcohol plunges you into weakness, into an irresistible need to find caresses, a vanished tenderness, the lost world of childhood, gratification, the need to find peace when faced with the glistering uncertainty of darkness.

You think you desire my beauty, the softness of my skin, the brilliance of my smile, the delicacy of my limbs, the crimson of my lips, but actually, what you want without realizing it is for your fears to disappear, for healing, union, return, oblivion. This power inside you devours you in solitude.

So you suffer, lost in an infinite twilight, one foot in day and the other in night.

THREE BUNDLES OF SABLE AND MINK FUR, ONE HUN-
dred and twelve *panni* of wool, nine rolls of Bergamo satin, the
same quantity of gilt Florentine velvet, five barrels of saltpeter,
two crates of mirrors, and one little jewelry box: that is the list
of things that disembark with Michelangelo Buonarroti in the
port of Constantinople on Thursday, May 13, 1506. Almost as
soon as the frigate moors, the sculptor leaps ashore. He sways
a little after six days of difficult sailing. No one knows the name
of the Greek dragoman waiting for him, so we'll call him Manuel; we do, however, know the name of the merchant accompa-
nying him: Giovanni di Francesco Maringhi, a Florentine who
has been living in Istanbul for five years now. The merchandise
belongs to him. He is a friendly man, happy to meet this hero of
the republic of Florence, the sculptor of *David*.

Of course Istanbul was very different then; it was known as
Constantinople; Hagia Sophia sat enthroned alone without the
Blue Mosque, the east bank of the Bosphorus was bare, the great
bazaar was not yet that immense spiderweb where tourists from
all over the world lose themselves so they can be devoured. The
Empire was no longer Roman and not really the Empire; the city
swayed between Ottomans, Greeks, Jews, and Latins; the Sultan
was named Bayezid the second, nicknamed the Holy, the Pious,
the Just. The Florentines and Venetians called him Bajazeto,

the French Bajazet. He was a wise, tactful man who reigned for thirty-one years; he loved wine, poetry, and music; he didn't turn his nose up at either men or women; he appreciated the arts and sciences, astronomy, architecture, the pleasures of war, swift horses, and sharp weapons. It is not known why he invited Michelangelo Buonarroti of the Buonarrotis of Florence to Istanbul, though certainly the sculptor was already enjoying great renown in Italy. Some saw him at the age of thirty-one as the greatest artist of the time. He was often compared to the immense Leonardo da Vinci, twenty years his senior.

THAT YEAR MICHELANGELO LEFT ROME ON A SUDDEN impulse, on Saturday April 17, the day before the laying of the first stone of the new Saint Peter's Basilica. He had gone for the fifth day in a row to request that the Pope deign to honor his promise of additional money. He was turned away each time.

Michelangelo Buonarroti shivers in his wool coat; the spring is timid, rainy. He reaches the borders of the republic of Florence as the clock strikes 2 a.m., Ascanio Condivi, his biographer, tells us; he stops over at an inn thirty leagues from the city.

Michelangelo rails against Julius II, the warlike, authoritarian pope who has treated him so poorly. Michelangelo is proud. Michelangelo is aware that he is an artist of great talent.

Knowing he is safe in Florentine territory, he turns away the attendants the Pope has sent after him with orders to bring him back to Rome, by force if necessary. He reaches Florence the next day in time for supper. His servant gives him a thin broth. Michelangelo curses the architect Bramante and the painter Raphael, those jealous types who, he thinks, have served him a bad turn with the Pope. Pontiff Julius Della Rovere is a proud man too. Proud, authoritarian, and a miser. The artist had to pay from his own pocket the cost of the marble that he went to pick out in Carrara to build the papal tomb, an immense monument that would sit enthroned right in the middle of the new basilica.

Michelangelo sighs. The advance on the contract signed by the Pope had been spent on furs, travel, and apprentices to quarry the blocks.

The sculptor, exhausted by the journey and his troubles, a little warmed by the broth, shuts himself away in his narrow Renaissance bed and falls asleep sitting up, his back against a cushion, because he is afraid of the image of death the outstretched position suggests.

THE NEXT DAY, HE WAITS FOR A MESSAGE FROM THE Pope. He trembles with rage when he thinks that the pontiff didn't even deign to receive him on the day before his departure. Bramante the architect is an imbecile, and Raphael the painter a pretentious ass. Two dwarfs who flatter the outrageous haughtiness of the crimson-robed one. Then Sunday arrives and Michelangelo eats meat for the first time in two months, a delicious lamb, cooked by his neighbor the baker.

He draws all day, runs through three red chalks and two graphite pencils in no time at all.

THE DAYS PASS, AND MICHELANGELO BEGINS TO WONder if he has made a mistake. He is hesitant to write a letter to His Holiness. Get back into favor and go back to Rome. Never. In Florence, the statue of *David* has made him the hero of the city. He could accept the commissions they won't fail to give him when they learn of his return, but that would unleash the fury of Julius, by whom he is employed. The idea of having to humiliate himself once more before the pontiff whips him into a frenzy.

He breaks two vases and a majolica plate.

Then, having calmed down, he begins drawing again, mainly anatomical studies.

Three days later, after vespers, writes Ascanio Condivi, he receives a visit from two Franciscan monks who arrive soaked from the pounding rain. The Arno has swollen a lot over the past few days; people are worried it will flood. The servant helps the monks dry off; Michelangelo observes the two men, their robes spotted with mud at the hem, their ankles bare, their calves thin.

"Maestro, we come to give you a message of the highest importance."

"How did you find me?"

Michelangelo thinks amusedly that Julius II has very mediocre envoys.

"Through your brother's directions, Maestro."

"Here is a letter for you, Maestro. It is a singular request, coming from a very high personage."

The letter is not stamped, but sealed in foreign characters. Michelangelo cannot help but feel disappointed when he sees that it does not come from the Pope. He puts the missive down on the table.

"What's it about?"

"It is an invitation from the Sultan of Constantinople, Maestro."

We can imagine the artist's surprise, his little eyes opening wide. The Sultan of Constantinople. The Great Turk. He turns the letter over in his hands. Vellum is one of the softest materials there is.

SITTING ON A BOAT IN THE WINDS OF THE ADRIATIC, Michelangelo is having regrets. His stomach is tied in knots, his ears are buzzing, he is afraid. This storm is divine vengeance. Off the coast of Ragusa, then off the Morea, he hears Saint Paul's phrase in his head: "To learn how to pray, you must go to sea," and he understands. The immensity of the watery plain frightens him. The deckhands speak a frightful nasal slang that he only half understands.

He left Florence on May 1 to take ship from Ancona, after six days of hesitation. The Franciscans came back three times, and three times he sent them away, asking them to wait some more. He read and reread the Sultan's letter, hoping that a sign from the Pope would in the meantime bring an end to his uncertainties. Julius II must have been too busy with his basilica and his preparations for another war. After all, serving the Sultan of Constantinople would be a fine revenge on the bellicose pontiff who had him thrown out like a beggar. And the sum offered by the Great Turk is astronomical. The equivalent of 50,000 ducats, five times what the Pope paid him for two years of work. One month. That's all Bayezid is asking for. One month to plan, draw, and start work on a bridge between Constantinople and Pera, the northern district. A bridge to cross what is called the Golden Horn, the *Khrusokeras* of the Byzantines. A bridge in the middle of Istanbul's harbor. A construction that will be over 900 feet long. Michelangelo half-heartedly tried to convince the Franciscans that he was not qualified. If the Sultan chose you, that's because you are qualified, Maestro, they replied. And if your drawing doesn't suit the Great Turk, he will reject it, just as he has already rejected the one by Leonardo da Vinci. Leonardo? Go after Leonardo da Vinci? After that oaf who scorns sculpture? The monk, without realizing it, immediately found the words that would convince Michelangelo: *You will surpass him in glory if you accept, for you will succeed where he has failed, and you will give the world a monument without equal, like your* David.

For now, leaning against a wet wooden rail, the peerless sculptor, future painter of genius, and immense architect, is nothing more than a body, twisted with fear and nausea.

ALL THESE FURS, THEN, ALL THESE WOOL PANNI, these rolls of Bergamo satin and Florentine velvet, these barrels and crates, landed after Michelangelo on May 13, 1506.

An hour earlier, passing the headland of the palace, the artist glimpsed Santa Sophia, the basilica, a broad-shouldered giant, an Atlas bearing its cupola to the summits of the known world; during the landing maneuvers, he observed the activity of the port; he watched the unloading of oil from Mytilene, soap from Tripoli, rice from Egypt, dried figs from Smyrna, salt and lead, silver, bricks and lumber for construction; he ran his eyes over the hills of the city, glimpsed the ancient seraglio, the minarets of a large mosque taller than the top of the hill; he looked especially at the opposite shore, the ramparts of the Galata Tower, on the other side of the Golden Horn, that estuary that looks so little like the mouth of the Tiber. So that's where, a little further upstream, he is supposed to build a bridge. The distance to cross is huge. How many arches should there be? How deep can this arm of the sea be?

Michelangelo and his luggage settle into a small room on the second floor of the Florentine merchant Maringhi's shops. They thought he'd prefer to board with his compatriots. His Greek dragoman is staying in a tiny room in a neighboring building. The room where Michelangelo Buonarroti unpacks his luggage looks out onto a passageway with beautiful stone arcades; a double row of windows, very tall, almost meeting the ceiling, distribute a light that seems to come from nowhere, diffracted by the wooden slats of the blinds. A bed and a chestnut table, an ornate walnut wardrobe, two oil lamps, and a heavy, round, cast-iron candelabrum hanging from the ceiling, and nothing more.

A small door hides a water closet tiled in multicolored faience that Michelangelo has no use for, since he never washes.

MICHELANGELO OWNS A NOTEBOOK, A SIMPLE NOTE-
book he made himself: some leaves of paper folded in half, held
together with a string, with a cover made of thick cardboard.
It's not a sketchbook, he doesn't draw in it; nor does he note
down the verses that come to him sometimes, or the drafts of
his letters, even less his impressions of the days or the weather
outside.

In this stained notebook, he records treasures. Endless ac-
cumulations of various objects, accounts, expenses, supplies;
clothes, menus, words, simply words.

His notebook is his sea chest.

The names of things give them life.

May 11, lateen sail, storm jib, topping lift, halyard, unfurling.

May 12, gasket, capstan, floor timber, gangway, keelson.

May 13, 1506, tow, tinder, tinder box, wick, wax, oil.

May 14, ten small sheets of heavy paper and five large ones,
three beautiful quill pens, one inkwell, one bottle of black ink,
one phial of red, some graphite, a lead holder, three pieces of
sanguine chalk.

Two ducats to Maringhi, skinflint, thief, cutthroat.

Fortunately the crust of bread and the coal are free.

FOR THE FIRST THREE DAYS, MICHELANGELO WAITS.
He rarely goes out, and mainly in the morning, not daring to wander away from the immediate surroundings of the stores of the Florentine who's hosting him. Manuel the translator accompanies him, offering to show him around the city, to visit the Basilica of Santa Sophia or the magnificent mosque that the Sultan Bayezid has just had built on a hill. Michelangelo refuses. He prefers his accustomed stroll: make a tour of the caravanserai, reach the port, walk alongside the ramparts up to the *porte della Farina*, as the Franks call it, look for a long time at the opposite shore of the Golden Horn, and return to his rooms. His guide follows him, silent. They hardly speak. Michelangelo for that matter speaks to no one. The artist usually takes his meals in his room.

He draws.

Michelangelo does not draw bridges.

He draws horses, men, and astragals.

HE DRAWS HORSES, MEN, AND ASTRAGALS FOR THREE days in a row, until the Grand Vizier finally sends for him. The Ottoman delegation is made up of a young page, a man from Genoa named Falachi, and a squad of janissaries wearing crimson turbans. They settle the sculptor in a grey and gold araba with a dashing harness; two spahis trot in front of the procession, to make way; their scimitars bump against the horses' flanks.

In the carriage, the page Falachi makes conversation; he explains how honored he is to find himself by the sculptor's side, how happy he is to meet him, and describes how impatient the court is finally to meet the immense artist who will carry out such a noble task. Michelangelo is surprised to discover a Genoese so close to the Grand Turk; Falachi smiles and explains he is a slave of the Sultan, captured at an early age by some corsairs, and that his position is an enviable one. He is powerful, well respected, and, if such things matter, rich. Manuel the Greek nods his head; Michelangelo opens the curtain covering the carriage window and watches the streets of Constantinople stream by to the rhythm of the convoy, often slowed down by porters or groups of traders. Warehouses overflowing with merchandise, wooden houses, Mohammedan churches whose clear terraces above the porches open eyes of light onto the body of the city.

The visit will be brief and short on protocol, Falachi explains.

The Vizier chiefly wants to introduce Michelangelo to those who will help him in his task, and to settle some administrative details that are nevertheless important. He will then be installed in a studio where he will find everything necessary for the exercise of his art—draftsmen, model-makers, and engineers.

Having arrived at the palace, the omnipresence of armed men reminds Michelangelo of his visits to Julius II, the warrior Pope. The vast courtyard where they step down from the carriage is both brilliant with sun and shaded. A crowd of janissaries and functionaries organize the arrivals. The buildings are low, new, dazzling; the artist can make out some stables, apartments, the palace guard; the passageways and hallways through which he is led are nothing like the dark, crumbling vaulted ceilings of the pontifical palace in Rome where neither Raphael nor Michelangelo himself have yet set brush.

The Grand Vizier's name is Ali Pasha; he receives visitors in a beautiful, ceremonial room decorated with ornate woodwork, faience, and calligraphy. It wasn't necessary to explain to Michelangelo that he should kneel before this imposing, turbaned man, one of the most powerful men in the known world, surrounded by a flock of scribes, secretaries, soldiers. Quickly, Falachi the page signals to the artist to come forward. The Vizier has a firm voice. He speaks a strange Italian, peppered with Genoese, Venetian, or perhaps Castilian. Maestro, we thank you for accepting the task that befalls you. Maestro Buonarroti, the Sultan, your great Lord Bayezid, rejoices to know you are among us.

Michelangelo lowers his eyes as a sign of respect and gratitude.

He can't help but imagine the reaction of Julius II when His Holiness the Very Christian Pope learns of this interview, and the presence of his favorite sculptor with the Grand Turk.

This thought instils in him a rather pleasant mixture of excitement and terror.

THE VIZIER ALI PASHA HAS A CONTRACT DELIVERED to Michelangelo in Latin, and a purse of 100 silver aspers for his expenses. The secretary who hands these papers over to him has soft hands and thin fingers; his name is Mesihi of Prishtina, and he is a well-read man, an artist, a great poet, protected by the Vizier. The face of an angel, a somber gaze, a sincere smile; he speaks a little Frankish, a little Greek; he knows Arabic and Persian. Then a series of dignitaries arrive: the *shehremini*, responsible for the city of Constantinople; the *mohendesbashi*, the chief engineer, who is not yet called Chief Architect; the *defterdar*, the bailiff; an abundance of servants. Falachi and Manuel translate the words of welcome and the encouragements of the crowd as quickly as they can; the sculptor is taken by the arm and led to the adjoining room, where a meal is set; already the uniformed pages half-hidden behind their long golden ewers are pouring scented water into tumblers. Michelangelo the frugal half-heartedly nibbles on the beef with dates, the stewed eggplant, the fowl with carob molasses; disoriented, he doesn't recognize the taste of cinnamon or camphor or mastic. The artist thinks all these people are ignoring him despite the sumptuousness of the reception; for them he is nothing but an image, a reflection without substance, and he feels slightly humiliated.

Michelangelo the divine has only one desire: to see the studio he has been promised, and get to work.

YOUR ARM IS HARD. YOUR BODY IS HARD. YOUR SOUL
is hard. Of course you're not sleeping. I know you were waiting
for me. I noticed you looking at me before. You knew I would
come. Everything is ordained. You desired my presence, I am
here. Many people would like to have me near them, lying in the
dark; you turn your back to me. I feel your tense muscles, the
muscles of a barbarian or a warrior. You must handle a sword to
have such strong arms. A sword or a scythe. I can't picture you
as a farmer, though, or a soldier, you wouldn't be here. You're
much too coarse to be a poet like your Turkish friend. So are
you a sailor, a captain, a merchant? I don't know. You weren't
looking at me like a thing that can be bought or possessed by
weapons.

I liked the way you observed me when I sang. The precision of
your eyes, the delicacy of their desire. And now what? Are you
afraid, foreigner? I'm the one who should be afraid. I'm nothing
but a voice in the darkness, I will disappear with the dawn. I will
slip out of this room when you can tell a black thread from a
white and when Muslims give the call to prayer.

They will pay me, you have nothing to feel guilty about. Let
yourself give in to pleasure. You're trembling. You don't desire
me? Then listen. Once upon a time, in a country far away . . . No,
I won't tell you a story. The time for stories has passed. The era
of fairy tales is over. The kings are savages who kill their horses

beneath them; it's been a long time since they offered elephants to their princesses. My world is dead, stranger, I had to flee it, abandon even my memories. I was a child. All I remember is the day of the fall, my panicked mother, my father, confident in the future, who tried to reassure her, our prince the traitor who fled after opening the city up to the Christian armies. It was in January, a soft snow was gleaming on the mountain. The weather was fine. Ysabel and Fernando, your coarse Catholic sovereigns, slept in the Alhambra; Fernando took off his armor to mount his royal female, in the most beautiful room in the palace, after sponsoring a victory Mass where all his knights, having entered the citadel without fighting, prayed fervently. Three months later, when we had seen the noble Spaniards settle in the medina, they chased us away. Departure, conversion, or death. We respected the Christians. There were pacts, agreements. Vanished overnight.

I'll probably never see the place where I grew up again. I could hate you for that, you and your cross. I'd have that right. My father died in the sufferings of the journey. My mother is buried two parasangs from here. Sultan Bayezid welcomed us, into this capital conquered by the Romans. That's justice. Eye for eye, city for city. You've stopped trembling. I'm caressing you gently and you remain icy, cold as a river. You don't like my story? I doubt you're really listening to me. You must understand some words, a few scraps, bits of phrases. You're surprised that I can speak Castilian. Many things would surprise you more if you had seen Grenada.

I have no bitterness. A pale winter sun shines down today on Andalusia, never will spring return there. Things pass.

They speak of a New World; they say that beyond the seas are infinitely wealthy lands that the Franks conquered. The stars are turning away from us; they are plunging us into twilight.

The light goes to the other side of the earth, who knows when it will return. I don't know you, stranger. You know nothing of me, we have only the night in common. We share this moment, despite ourselves. Despite the blows we have brought against each other, the things destroyed, I am pressed against you in the dark. I will not entertain you with my stories till dawn. I will speak to you neither of good genies nor terrifying ghouls, nor of journeys to dangerous islands. Let yourself go. Forget your fear, take advantage of the fact that I, like you, am a piece of flesh that belongs to no one except God. Take a little of my beauty, the perfume of my skin. I'm offering it to you. It will be neither a betrayal nor a vow; neither a defeat nor a victory.

Just two hands imprisoning each other, the way lips press against each other without ever joining.

MANUEL THE TRANSLATOR VISITS MICHELANGELO EV-
ery morning to ask him if he needs anything, if he can accompany him anywhere; usually he finds the sculptor busy drawing, or else compiling one of his countless lists in his notebook.
Sometimes, he is fortunate enough to be able to observe the
Florentine as he outlines, in ink or graphite, an anatomical
study, or the detail of an architectural ornament.

Manuel is fascinated.

Amused by his interest, Michelangelo shows off. He asks him
to place his hand on the table and, in two minutes, he sketches
the wrist, all the complexity of the curved fingers and the flesh
of the fingers.

"It's a miracle, Maestro," Manuel whispers.

Michelangelo bursts out laughing.

"A miracle? No, my friend. It's pure genius, I don't need God
for that."

Manuel remains stunned.

"I'm making fun of you, Manuel. It's work, above all. Talent is
nothing without work. Try it, if you like."

Manuel shakes his head, terrified.

"But I don't know how, Maestro, I know nothing about drawing."

"I'll teach you. There's no other way. Lean your left arm on the table in front of you, with your hand half-open, thumb relaxed, and with your right hand draw what you see, once, twice, three times, a thousand times. You don't need a model or a master. There is everything in one hand. Bones, movements, materials, proportions, even drapery. Trust your eye. Begin again until you know how. Then you'll do the same thing with your foot, placing it on a stool; then with your face, with the help of a mirror. Only then can you move on to a model, for the poses."

"You think it's possible to get there, Maestro? Here no one draws like you. Icons . . ."

Michelangelo interrupts him abruptly.

"Icons are children's images, Manuel. Painted by children for children. Believe me, follow my advice and you'll see that you can draw. Afterward you can amuse yourself by copying icons as much as you like."

"I'll try, Maestro. Would you like to go for a walk or visit a monument?"

"No, Manuel, not now. I'm fine here, the light is perfect, there are no shadows on my page, I'm working, I don't need anything else, thank you."

"All right. Tomorrow we'll go see your studio. See you soon, then."

And the Greek dragoman withdraws, wondering if he'll dare to place his hand on the table and begin drawing too.

THE STUDIO IS IN THE OUTBUILDINGS OF THE FOR-
mer palace of the sultans, a stone's throw from a grandiose
mosque whose construction has just been completed. The sec-
retary-poet Mesihi, the page Falachi and Manuel accompanied
Michelangelo to take possession of the site, a little worried
about the artist's reaction.

A tall, vaulted room, furnished with a crowd of draftsmen
and engineers, standing in rows in front of large tables cluttered
with drawings and plans.

Some models on display stands, several different models of
strange workmanship, a singular bridge, two parabolas that
form a deck at their asymptote, supported by a single arch, a
little like a cat arching its back.

Here are your kingdom and your subjects, Maestro, Falachi
says. Mesihi adds a phrase of welcome that Michelangelo does
not hear. His gaze is fixed on the models.

"They are models made from the drawing proposed by Leonardo da Vinci, Maestro. The engineers thought it inventive, but
impossible to build and, how to put it, the Sultan thought it
rather . . . rather ugly, despite its lightness."

If the great Leonardo understood nothing of sculpture, then
he understands nothing of architecture either.

Michelangelo the genius walks over to the project of his famous elder; he looks at it for a minute, then, with a broad swipe, propels it to the bottom of the pedestal; the glued-wood edifice falls on its feet without breaking.

The sculptor then places his right shoe on the small-scale model and crushes it furiously.

The bridge over the Golden Horn must unite two fortresses, it is a royal bridge, a bridge that, from two shores that everything keeps apart, will form a huge city. Leonardo da Vinci's drawing is ingenious. Leonardo da Vinci's drawing is so innovative that it is frightening. Leonardo da Vinci's drawing is devoid of interest because he is thinking neither of the Sultan, nor of the city, nor of the fortress. Instinctively, Michelangelo knows he will go much further, that he will succeed, because he has seen Constantinople, because he has understood that the work demanded of him is not a vertiginous footbridge, but the cement of a city, of the city of emperors and sultans. A military bridge, a commercial bridge, a religious bridge.

A political bridge.

A piece of urbanity.

The engineers, model-makers, Mesihi, Falachi, and Manuel all have their eyes riveted on Michelangelo, the way one looks at a bomb whose fuse has been lit. They wait for the artist to calm down.

Which he does. His eyes sparkle, he smiles, he looks as if he has just emerged from an overstimulating dream.

He shoves the model's debris away with his foot, then says calmly:

"This studio is magnificent. To work. Manuel, take me to see the Santa Sophia Basilica, please."

ON MAY 18, 1506, MICHELANGELO BUONARROTI, standing on the short esplanade, looks at the church that, just fifty years earlier, was still the center of Christianity. He thinks of Constantine, of Justinian, of the imperial purple, and of the more or less barbaric crusaders that have entered it on horseback to emerge loaded down with relics; twenty years later, drawing a dome for the Basilica of St. Peter in Rome, he would think again of the cupola of that Santa Sophia whose profile he can see from the square where the people of Istanbul crowd together for afternoon prayer, guided by the human clock of the muezzin.

Next to him, Mesihi, native son of Prishtina, perhaps also remembers his emotion when he first arrived in Constantinople, in Istanbul, the newly appointed residence of the Sultan and capital of the Empire; in any case, he takes the sculptor by the arm and says, pointing to the faithful passing through the building's vast narthex:

"Let's follow them, Maestro."

And Michelangelo, aided by the poet's hand and the fascination exercised on him by the sublime edifice, overcomes his fear and distaste for Muslim things and enters it.

THE SCULPTOR HAS NEVER SEEN ANYTHING LIKE IT.
Eighteen pillars of the most beautiful marble, serpentine tiles and porphyry inlays, four perfect arches that bear a vertiginous dome. Mesihi leads him upstairs to the gallery overlooking the prayer hall. Michelangelo has eyes only for the cupola and especially for the windows through which pours a sun divided into squares, a joyful light that outlines imageless icons on the walls.

Such an impression of lightness despite the mass, such a contrast between the outer austerity and the elevation, the levitation almost, of the inner space, the balance of proportions in the magical simplicity of the square design in which the circle of the dome fits perfectly, it nearly brings tears to the sculptor's eyes. If only his master Giuliano da Sangallo were here. The old Florentine architect would no doubt immediately begin drawing, bringing out details, plotting elevations.

Below him, in the choir, the faithful are prostrating on countless rugs. They kneel down, place their foreheads on the ground, then get up, look at their hands held out in front of them as if they were holding a book, then place them behind their ears the better to hear a silent clamor, and then they kneel down again. They are murmuring, chanting, and the hum of all these inaudible words buzzes and mingles with the pure light, without any pious images, without any sculptures to divert the gaze from God; just a few arabesques, snakes of blank ink, seem to float in the air.

Strange beings, these Mohammedans.

Strange beings, these Mohammedans and their austere cathedral, without even an image of their Prophet. Through Manuel, Mesihi explains to Michelangelo that the white plaster coats hide the Christian mosaics and frescos that used to cover the walls. Calligraphies are our images, Maestro, images of our faith. Manuel deciphers the barbaric writing for the artist: There is no god but God, Mohammed is the prophet of God.

"Here, Mohammed is the one you call Maometto, Maestro."

The one Dante sends to the fifth circle of Hell, thinks Michelangelo, before resuming his contemplation of the building.

Constantinople, May 19, 1506
  To Buonarroto di Lodovico di Buonarrota Simoni in Firenze

Buonarroto, I received today, May 19, a letter from you in which you recommend Piero Aldobrandini and enjoin me to do what he asks of me. Know that he has written to me here requesting I make him a dagger blade, and that I make a special effort for it to be marvelous. I don't know how I could serve him quickly and well: first of all because that is not at all my profession, and second because I have no time to devote to it. However I will strive to satisfy him in one way or another.

For your affairs, especially those of Giovan Simone, I understood everything. I would like him to set himself up in your shop, for I want to help him just as much as the rest of you; and if God grant me his aid, as he always has up till now, I hope to have finished rather quickly what I must do here and will return to do what I promised you. For the money you say Giovan Simone wants to invest in a trade, you should urge him to wait until I return, and we will settle everything all together. I know you understand me, and that is enough. Tell him from me that if he still wants the sum you mention, he'll have to take it from the Santa Maria Maggiore account. From here I have nothing to send you yet because I've only acquired a little money from my work, which is still a doubtful thing, and which could cause my ruin. For that reason I ask you to be patient for a little while, until I return.

As for Giovan Simone's wish to join me, I do not advise it for the moment, for I'm staying here in a mean chamber, so I would not have the possibility of receiving him as he should be. If he insists, tell him one can't come here in a day on horseback!

That's all.

Pray to God for me and for everything to go well.

Your Michelagnolo

MAY 19: CANDLES, LAMP, TWO SMALL COINS; POTTAGE (herbs, spices, bread, oil) the same; fried fish, two pigeons, one ducat and a half; plates & cutlery, one small coin; wool blanket, one ducat.

Clear, cool water.

A LUTE, A MANDOLA, AND A VIOL THAT MICHELAN-
gelo does not know are called *oud, saz,* and *kaman,* accompanied by a tambourine played with fingers alternately caressing
and violent by a young woman dressed as a man, whose metal
bracelets jingle in rhythm and from time to time, adding a me-
tallic percussion to the concert and distracting the Florentine
artist a little from this music that's both wild and melancholic:
it is with this accompaniment that the young woman — or the
young man, it would be hard to swear to the sex, thanks to the
harem trousers and billowing shirt — sings poems of which Michelangelo can make nothing. Between couplets, as the little
orchestra is playing to its heart's content, she, or he, dances;
an elegant dance, very restrained, in which the body spins,
moves around a fixed axis, almost without the feet moving at
all. A slow undulation of strings released, manipulated by the
wind. If it's a woman's body, it's perfect; if it's a man's body, Michelangelo would pay dearly to see the muscles of his thighs
and calves stand out, his bone structure moving, his shoulders
animating his biceps and pectorals. At times, the baggy trousers allow glimpses of a thin but powerful ankle, twisted by the
effort; the shirt, which stops below the elbow, before the bracelets, rhythmically reveals the muscles of the forearm jutting
out, which the sculptor cherishes as the most beautiful part of

the body, on which you can most easily imprint movement, expression, will.

Little by little, sitting crosslegged on his cushions, Michelangelo feels overwhelmed with emotion. His ears forget the music, or else perhaps it's the music itself that is plunging him into this state, making his eyes tremble and filling them with tears that will not flow; as it was on that afternoon at Santa Sophia, as it is every time he touches Beauty, or approaches it, the artist shivers with happiness and suffering intermingled.

Next to Michelangelo, Mesihi observes him; he sees him overcome by this pleasure of the body and soul together that only Art, or perhaps opium and wine, can offer, and he smiles, happy to discover that the foreign guest is moved by the rhythm of the androgynous jewels to which he keeps his eyes riveted.

After the visit to the Basilica, Michelangelo wanted to rest a little, not without first giving an order to his team, which Manuel hurried to transmit: I absolutely have to have the plans and diagrams of Santa Sophia, the sections and elevations. There is nothing easier, he was assured, but to what purpose? The sculptor remained evasive. Then he withdrew into the sobriety of his room, absorbed by paper and pen until the always surprising voices of those human church bells on top the minarets confirm for him, along with the shadows lengthening on his page, that the sun has just set. He had written two letters, one to his brother Buonarroto in Florence, to give him instructions about his younger brother Giovan Simone, and the other to Giuliano da Sangallo in Rome, mail that he will entrust the next day to the merchant Maringhi. No sooner had he folded them up than Manuel knocked on his door to announce the visit of Mesihi of Prishtina, who wanted to invite him to a private concert; afterwards, they'd drink and dine, if they were so moved. Michelangelo hesitated, but the gentle insistence of the interpreter and poet as well as the possible presence of the Grand Vizier Ali Pasha in person made up his mind.

So he let himself be led by foot through the warm city streets. Shops were closing and craftsmen were finishing their work; the perfume of rose and jasmine, augmented by evening, mingled with the sea air and the less poetic effluvia of the city. The sculptor, still dazzled by his afternoon visit, was surprisingly talkative. He explained to Mesihi how much Constantinople reminded him of Venice, which he had visited ten years before; there was something of Santa Sophia in St. Mark's Basilica, something that expressed itself confusedly, stifled by the pillars, something the artist couldn't really describe—perhaps just the illusion of memory. Mesihi asked him about Rome, about Florence, about the poets and artists; Michelangelo spoke of Dante and Petrarch, unsurpassable geniuses of whom neither Manuel nor Mesihi had ever heard; of Lorenzo the Magnificent, the sorely missed patron of the Arts who had transformed Florence. The conversation moved on to Leonardo da Vinci, the only person Manuel and Mesihi could cite; Michelangelo tried to explain to them that the old man was detestable, ready to sell himself to any purse, to help any army at war, with ideas from another time on Art and the nature of things. Mesihi told how at the beginning of his reign, Sultan Bayezid had been at war with the Pope because of his brother Djem, the renegade rival, who had taken refuge in Italy, in Rome at first, then with the King of Naples, and how that war had been followed by another one, with the Republic of Venice. The Empire had only maintained peace with the ruling powers of Italy for a few years.

They arrived at a barred door in the middle of a tall windowless wall, a door in which a Judas hole quickly opened. A servant led them into a courtyard garden lit by torches. In a room with a wooden ceiling that overlooked this courtyard, cushions and rugs had been set up. The guests were served scented drinks and chilled fruits. Then other guests arrived; among them the Vizier Ali Pasha and his inseparable Genoese page; they greeted Michelangelo with a detachment the artist thought humiliating.

The concert began, the sculptor was moved, and now he is unsure about applauding the female or male dancer who has just finished his or her extraordinary show. But he restrains himself, seeing that the audience is content to resume its chatter without any mark of admiration. Mesihi turns to him and asks, smiling, in his strange Frankish, if the spectacle was to his taste. The Florentine passionately agrees, even though he has never been interested in music, probably because music at home is nothing but a sad activity for monks, and dance the work of trained bears or peasant revelers.

Incapable of following the discussions in Turkish, Michelangelo, still trembling with emotion, continues his contemplation of the dancer (he is more and more convinced that it's a man and not a woman) who has sat down crosslegged among the musicians, a few feet away. He only looks away, embarrassed, when that beauty smiles at him. Fortunately he doesn't need to hide his embarrassment. Mesihi has got up, in the murmuring of the spectators. Standing, he begins to recite some verses: a harmonious, rhythmic melody of which Michelangelo only understands the assonances. The lute accompanies the poet at times; sometimes the audience punctuates the ends of the verses with long, drawn-out *ahs*, sighs, admiring murmurs.

When Mesihi sits back down, Manuel vainly tries to translate what they've just heard; Michelangelo grasps only that it was about love, drunkenness, and cruelty.

IN THE BEWILDERED SOLITUDE OF SOMEONE WHO knows nothing of the language, the codes, the customs of the gathering in which he is taking part, Michelangelo feels empty, the object of attentions that he doesn't understand. Mesihi is sitting next to him again; Ali Pasha provoked the tumultuous joy of the assembly by uttering—almost singing—these mysterious words, Sâqi biyâ bar khiz o mey biyâr, followed immediately by an effect: a servant distributed blue-tinted cups, Manuel explained the obvious, *Come, cupbearer, get up and bring the wine*, and with a magical step, with a gesture that made the heavy copper vase seem to weigh nothing, the light-bodied male or female dancer filled the glasses one after the other, beginning with the Vizier's. Michelangelo the genius trembled when the loose fabric and tense muscles came so close to him and, although he never drinks, now he brings the cup to his lips, in a sign of gratitude to his hosts and in homage to the beauty of the man or woman who served him this thick, spiced wine. A cypress when standing, he or she is a willow when, leaning over the drinker, the cupbearer tilts the container from which the dark liquid flows, gleaming red in the lamplight, sapphires vying with rubies.

The guests formed a circle, the musicians kept themselves apart. The dancer sits down to become a singer again when the glasses are empty. Fascinated by the powerful voice that soars so easily in the treble range, Michelangelo is not listening to the translator's explanation as he exhausts himself commenting on the song. This second intoxication — of the gentleness of the features, the ivory teeth between coral lips, the expression of fragile hands placed on knees — is stronger than the heady wine he swallows in great gulps, in the hope that he will be served again, that this so-perfect creature might approach him again.

Which is what happens, and happens again between song after song for hours on end until, conquered by so many pleasures and by wine, the sober Michelangelo dozes off in the hollow of his cushions, like a child rocked too well.

A maestro Giuliano da Sangallo, architetto del papa in Roma

Giuliano, I learned from one of your letters that the Pope has taken offence at my absence and that His Holiness is ready to put up the money and do everything we had agreed upon, that he desires my return and wants me to have no doubts.

Concerning my departure from Rome, the truth is that I heard the Pope saying, on Holy Saturday, over lunch, speaking with a jeweler and the master of ceremonies, that he didn't want to spend a penny more on stones, large or small: which surprised me greatly. Before leaving him, I asked for what I needed to continue my work. His Holiness told me to come back on Monday: I went back on Monday and Tuesday and Wednesday and Thursday, all in vain. Finally, on Friday morning, I was led away, or rather chased away, and the one who threw me out told me he knew who I was, but that he had received his orders.

So, since I had heard the aforementioned words on Saturday, and seen their effect, I became full of despair. But that was not the only cause for my departure, there is also another affair, which I don't want to write down here; suffice it to say that, if I had remained in Rome, they would have erected my tomb before the Pope's. That is the reason for my sudden move.

You write to me now on behalf of the Pope, and no doubt you will read these words to him: may His Holiness know that I am more than ever ready to finish the work. It has been over five years now that we have been in agreement on the sepulcher, it will be in St. Peter's and as beautiful as I promised: I am sure that, if it is done, there will be no equal to it in all the world.

I beg you then, my dearest Giuliano, to send me the reply.
Nothing else.

This day, May 19, 1506,
Your Michelagnolo, sculptor in Florence

THE SOBER MICHELANGELO DOZED OFF NESTLED IN
his cushions and wakes up alone and full of misery in his wooden
bed. Shreds of a nightmare seal his lids shut. He vaguely remembers that Mesihi and Manuel brought him back in a carriage or
a sedan chair and threw him onto his bed. Shame grips him.
He clenches his teeth. Pulls at his beard to tear it out. The pain
of remorse is so great that he takes refuge in prayer. *Dear God,
forgive all my sins, dear God, forgive me for being among infidels, dear
God, free me from temptation and keep me from evil.*

Then he gets up, staggering, as when he disembarked from
the boat a few days before; he decides to go back to Florence
as soon as possible. No doubt he is afraid; perhaps he sees the
furious Pope leaning over him, threatening excommunication;
he thinks of the Last Judgement: he will join Mohammed in one
of the circles of Hell, where he will be torn limb from limb and
disemboweled for eternity, in the midst of devils and demons.

But wasn't it the Pope himself who provoked this departure?
Didn't God will it? Didn't His Holiness have him chased out like
an undesirable, and what's more without paying him? Only his
brothers know he's in Constantinople. He has been hiding his
visit for now and has his other letters postmarked in Florence,
through the merchant Maringhi, whom he has asked for the
greatest discretion. Even if they know he's no longer in Tus-

cany, they'd think he was in Bologna, Venice, Milan, even, but certainly not with the Great Turk.

Just this once won't hurt, the sculptor goes to the bathroom and, as much to wash away his anxieties as to erase the effects of the heavy wine from the night before, he splashes his face with freezing water. Then, having regained his calm, he knots a piece of cloth around his head like a turban, out of habit, as artists do to protect themselves from marble dust or pigment spatters. Did he do this because he was thinking of the sculptures on the tomb of Julius II, out of simple habit, or to ward off the effects of a migraine, as if his heart were beating faster in his brain dulled by wine, which stiffens the neck as thoroughly as starch? Probably all of those reasons at once.

When someone knocks on his door, the sculptor is sitting at his table, sketching from memory the ankles and calves of the cupbearer from the night before with swift, thin lines; he couldn't remember his name; Mesihi told him something about where he came from, his distant origins, which he forgot too. He regretfully raises his eyes from his drawing.

"Mesihi of Prishtina is here, Maestro."

The visit is announced by the merchant Maringhi's servant, who brings him a broth of innards and a piece of bread.

"I'll come out and eat downstairs."

He puts on a tunic and shoes, emerges onto the gallery, walks to the stairway and reaches the courtyard. Mesihi is waiting for him, sitting on a stool in the shade of the tall fig tree. The sky of Istanbul is extraordinarily blue that morning, pure color spread all the way out to the stones of the caravanserai, right against the leaves of the tree, with their green so dense.

The servant pulls up another stool, a wooden crate, two dishes of steaming bouillon, a piece of brown bread, and a few sprouts of spring garlic.

Mesihi rose when he saw Michelangelo approaching and greeted him gracefully. Elegantly dressed, with a brilliant smile and a towering silhouette, the poet took care to add a little makeup to his eyes, probably to hide the effects of debauchery and lack of sleep. In the absence of the dragoman Manuel to communicate, the two men have to be content with the rudiments of Frankish that Mesihi knows. Michelangelo tries to speak slowly and to articulate; this language probably reminds Mesihi of the Italian merchants of his childhood, the Dalmatian intonations of his mother, a Christian captured in Ragusa. They speak neither of Art nor of poetry or architecture, but of how the soup tastes, the loveliness of the day; for different reasons, neither one mentions the night before. Lunch over, the servant brings over a copper pitcher and pours water on their hands.

Joined by a draftsman and an engineer, the great artist and the Vizier's favorite poet leave the storerooms of Maringhi the Florentine to go to the port.

MICHELANGELO NOTES THE NAMES OF THE MERCHANdise even though he does not know the names of the vessels of all sizes that carry them, in a hurry to deposit their cargo and make room for other crafts—oil from Mytilene, soap from Tripoli, rice from Egypt, molasses from Crete, cloth from Italy, coal from Izmit, stones from the Bosphorus.

During the rest of the morning, on the quays around the gate in the city's ramparts and as far as the middle of the harbor where they are ferried in a skiff, Michelangelo and the engineers observe and measure. The Florentine sculptor contemplates the landscape, the fortified hill of Pera on the other side of the Golden Horn, the glory of Stambul facing him; the surveyors calculate the exact breadth of the arm of the sea, show the artist the precise place planned for the bridge. They discuss units of distance, Florentine or Venetian cubits, Ottoman *kulaç* and *endazeh*; finally they disembark on the other shore, that district so steep that the towers defending it seem parallel to the slope.

Strange beings, these Mohammedans, so tolerant of Christian things. Pera is populated mainly by Latins and Greeks, there are many churches. A few Jews and Moors from far-off Andalusia stand out mainly by their dress. All those who refused to become Christian have recently been ejected from Spain.

The visit over, the measurements taken, the artist expresses the wish to go back to Constantinople to start drawing again.

49

IT BEGINS WITH THE PROPORTIONS. ARCHITECTURE is the art of equilibrium; just as the body is ruled by precise laws — length of arms, of legs, position of muscles — a building obeys rules that guarantee its harmony. The arrangement of things is the key to a façade, the beauty of a temple stems from the order, the articulation of the elements with respect to one another. A bridge will be the cadence of the arches, their curve, the elegance of the pilings, the wings, the deck. Recesses, glyphs, ornaments to mark the transitions will indeed be there, but already, in the relationship between vaults and pillars, everything will be expressed.

Michelangelo has no ideas.

This work must be unique, a masterpiece of grace, like *David*, like the *Pietà*.

Sketching out his first drafts, he thinks of Leonardo da Vinci, so unlike him, as if they were living in two eras separated by an infinity of eons.

Michelangelo stands gaping on his platform. He cannot yet see this bridge. He is drowning in the details. He has only a little experience in architecture; the sketches of Julius' tomb are his most architectural work to date. He would like Sangallo to be with him. He regrets having agreed to take up this challenge. He is upset. The risk is enormous. They might not only know he's here, but they could get to him too. He doesn't doubt for an instant that the Pope's iron hand, or deadly Roman conspiracies, could strike him wherever they see fit.

A giant bridge between two fortresses.

A fortified bridge.

Michelangelo knows that ideas come to you through drawing; he keeps outlining shapes, arches, pilings.

The space between the ramparts and the shore is small.

He thinks of the old medieval bridge of Florence, that frog surmounted by crenellations and peopled with butcher shops stinking of corpses, narrow, closed in on itself, it lets you see neither the majesty of the river, nor the grandeur of the city. He remembers the blood flowing in the Arno in rivulets when the animals are slaughtered; he has always had a horror of that bridge.

The amplitude of the task frightens him.

Leonardo's drawing obsesses him. It is vertiginous, but flawed. Empty. Lifeless. Lacking ideals. Decidedly Leonardo takes himself for Archimedes and forgets beauty. Beauty comes from abandoning the refuge of the old forms for the uncertainty of the present. Michelangelo is not an engineer. He is a sculptor. They sent for him so that a form could be born from matter, be drawn, be revealed.

For now, the matter of the city is so obscure to him that he doesn't know what tool to use to attack it.

MICHELANGELO HAS INTRODUCED A NEW RITUAL into his half-idle life, along with the daily stroll with Mesihi: he asks Manuel to read to him. Every day after noon the dragoman joins him and sight-translates poems for him, Turkish or Persian stories, Greek or Latin treatises that they choose together in the beautiful brand-new library that—by royal privilege—Bayezid opened to the artist.

Decidedly these Ottomans are masters of light. Bayezid's library, like his mosque, on a hill, is bathed in an omnipresent but discreet sunlight, whose rays never fall directly on the readers. You need all the attention of a Michelangelo to discover, in the knowledgeable game of placement and orientation of windows, the secret of the miraculous harmony of this simple space whose majesty, instead of crushing the visitor, places him at the center of the arrangement, flatters him, exalts and reassures him.

Michelangelo's curiosity is boundless.

Everything interests him.

He chooses unknown manuscripts, narratives he knows nothing about; he has Manuel read him *The Symposium*, and is amused by Socrates's games, the sandals he wore to keep from dirtying his feet, since he wanted to look handsome to go drinking at Agathon's; scholarly treatises mostly interest him for the stories they contain.

For example, of *The Elements* by Vitruvius, the only known ancient treatise on architecture, Michelangelo will remember much more clearly Dinocrates's anecdote than the considerations on the proportions of temples or urban planning. *Dinocrates, counting on his experience and skill, set off one day from Macedonia to go to the army of Alexander, who was then master of the world, and to whom he wanted to make himself known. Leaving his country, he had brought letters of recommendation from his parents and friends to the most distinguished personages of the court, in order to have easier access to the king. Having been kindly received by them, he asked to be presented as soon as possible to Alexander. The promise was made; but the execution took time: a favorable opportunity had to be found. Suspecting they were making fun of him, Dinocrates took matters into his own hands. He was tall, his face pleasant. In him beauty was joined with great dignity. These presents of nature filled him with confidence. He left his clothes at his inn, rubbed his body with oil, crowned himself with a poplar branch, then, covering his left shoulder with a lion's skin and arming his right hand with a club, he headed for the tribunal where the king was handing out justice. The novelty of the spectacle drew the attention of the crowd. Alexander saw Dinocrates, and, struck with surprise, ordered them to let him approach, and asked him who he was. "I am the architect Dinocrates," he replied; "Macedonia is my homeland. The models and plans I present to Alexander are worthy of his greatness. I gave to Mount Athos the shape of a man who, in his left hand, holds the enclosure of a city, and in his right, a cup where the waters of all the rivers that emerge from the mountain flow in, before they spread to the sea."*

Lying on his wooden bed, Michelangelo listens enraptured to Manuel's hesitant voice. This Dinocrates is ingenious.

Since the dawn of time people have had to humiliate themselves before the Caesars.

He pictures himself facing Julius II, wearing an animal skin, club in hand, and can't help but burst out laughing.

MAY 20: PEPPERCORNS, CINNAMON STICKS, NUTMEG, camphor, dried peppers, saffron pistils, rupturewort, agrimony, powdered cinnamon, cumin, euphorbia and mandrake from the Orient, all at just two aspers for four full ounces — you could make a fortune in this trade.

Michelangelo spent the day strolling around the city and its bazaars in the company of the poet Mesihi. The sculptor is surprised he gets along so well with an infidel. Their friendship is as strong as it is discreet.

Mesihi took Michelangelo far south, beyond the walls of Byzantium, to a strange open-air market, the market of live bodies, of men and animals. Michelangelo observed with terror the thin bodies of black slaves from Ethiopia, the white women taken from the Caucasus or Bulgaria, caravans of the wretched roped to each other, waiting for a better fate in the home of a wealthy Istanbul native or on a construction site. He quickly averted his eyes from the misery of his coreligionists.

The animals were even more impressive.

All of creation was there, or almost all. Oxen, sheep, golden horses from Turkmenistan, sorrels, Arab steeds as black as night, short-haired dromedaries, camels with long woolen coats, and, in one corner, the rarest mammals, from far-off India via Persia.

Mesihi was greatly amused by the Florentine's astonishment.

Two little elephants were trumpeting, leaning against their mother.

Michelangelo wanted to go over and stroke them.

"They say that brings luck, Mesihi."

The poet laughed when he saw the artist venture into the mud to touch the rough skin of the huge animals with the tips of his fingers.

"Do you want one?"

The Florentine pictured for an instant the look on the face of the skinflint Maringhi upon discovering an elephant in his courtyard, washing itself in his fountain. An entirely pleasing prospect.

"I couldn't forgive myself for inflicting on this sumptuous animal the meagre fare my host serves, Mesihi."

"That's very true, Maestro. Look, I found something that would suit you better."

In a tall metal cage, a tiny fawn-colored monkey, hand in its mouth, was mistrustfully observing the poet. At the sight of Michelangelo, it began executing a little dance, then hung from the bars by its tail, and finally fell gracefully back to the ground and saluted, like an artist after a performance.

Michelangelo applauded, laughing.

"He can recognize an appreciative audience, apparently," said Mesihi, mockingly.

"You're right. What's more, his goatee gives him a very serious air. He is a noble monkey, worthy of a high-ranking person."

"He is my present to you, then. He can keep you company as you work."

Michelangelo didn't think the offer was serious, and so didn't protest; when he found himself with the cage in his hand, it was too late.

"It's too kind, you shouldn't have. His company will remind me of yours," he added, in a honeyed voice.

Mesihi, disconcerted for a few seconds, burst out in a loud laugh when he saw the wicked smile on the artist's mouth.

Now the animal is gamboling joyfully in his room, leaping onto the bed, onto the table, hanging from the open door of his apartment, pouncing on a seed, coming over to Michelangelo to disturb him in his note-taking.

This energy delights him.

He watches the monkey for a long time the way a child looks at an unpredictable mobile, before plunging back into his countless sketches of bridges.

AT FIRST SIGHT MESIHI'S IS A VERY DIFFERENT ART: the height of the letter, the thickness of the line that gives movement, the disposition of the consonants, space stretching out according to sounds. Clinging to his reed pen, the calligrapher-poet gives a face to words, to phrases, to lines or verses. He is known to have drawn miniatures as well, but none of these images seems to have survived, unless one of them is still sleeping in a forgotten manuscript. Scenes of drinking bouts, faces, gardens where lovers are lying down while fantastical animals fly over them, illustrations of great mystical poems or courtly romances: an anonymous painter, Mesihi signs only his verses, which are few; he prefers pleasures — wine, opium, flesh — over the austere temptation of posterity. He is often found drunk, leaning against the wall of the tavern, at dawn; people shake him and then he needs to sweat for a long time in the steam bath, massaging his temples, to return to his body. Mesihi loved men and women, women and men, sang the praises of his patron and the delights of spring, both sweet and full of despair at the same time; he had no more experience with fatherhood or even marriage than Michelangelo did; unlike Michelangelo, he found no consolation in faith, even though he appreciated the aquatic calm of the courtyards of mosques and the fraternal chant of the muezzin on top of the minaret. Above all he loved the city, the noisy dens where the Janissaries drank, the activity of the port, the accents of foreigners.

And, more than anything, he loved drawing, the black wound of the ink, that caress scraping the grain of the paper.

YOUR DRUNKENNESS IS SO SWEET TO ME THAT IT IN-
toxicates me.

You are breathing gently. You are alive. I would like to move
over to your side of the world, see into your dreams. Are you
dreaming of a white, fragile love over there, so far away? Of
a childhood, a lost palace? I know I don't have a place there;
none of us will have a place there. You are closed in like a shell.
It would be so easy, though, for you to open up, a tiny crack
where life could rush in. I can guess your fate. You will remain
in the light, they will celebrate you, you will be rich. Your name,
immense as a fortress, will hide us with its shadow. They will
forget what you have seen here. These moments of time will
disappear. You yourself will forget my voice, the body you desired, your tremblings, your hesitations. I would so like for you
to keep something of it. For you to carry away a part of me. So
that something of my far-off homeland could be passed on. Not
a vague memory, an image, but the energy of a star, its vibration
in the dark. A truth. I know that men are children who chase
away their despair with anger, their fear with love; they respond
to the void by building castles and temples. They cling to stories,
they shove them in front of them like banners; everyone makes
some story his own so as to attach himself to the crowd that
shares it. You conquer people by telling them of battles, kings,

elephants, and marvelous beings; by speaking to them about the happiness they will find beyond death, the bright light that presided over their birth, the angels wheeling around them, the demons menacing them, and love, love, that promise of oblivion and satiety. Tell them about all of that, and they will love you; they will make you the equal of a god. But you will know, since you are here pressed against me, you ill-smelling Frank whom chance has brought to my hands, you will know that all this is nothing but a perfumed veil hiding the eternal suffering of night.

MAY 22: CIPOLIN, OPHITE, SARRANCOLIN, SERPEN-tine, canela, delfino, porphyry, brocatello, obsidian, marble from Cinna. So many names, colors, materials, whereas the most beautiful, the only one worth anything, is white, white, white without veins, grooves or colorations.

He misses marble.

Its softness in hardness. The delicate strength you need to work it, the time it takes you to polish it.

Michelangelo quickly shuts his notebook when Manuel enters his room without knocking.

"Maestro, excuse me, but we were worried."

Michelangelo puts down his quill.

"Why, Manuel? What worries you so much?"

Manuel suddenly seems embarrassed. Without a doubt this Florentine is mysterious.

"But Maestro, your lamp burned all night long, and you've eaten nothing since yesterday morning."

The monkey seems to be listening attentively to the conversation from his perch.

The sculptor sighs.

"That's true, you are right. Now that you tell me that, I think I'm hungry."

The young Greek seems immediately reassured.

"I can have a meal sent up to you, if you like."

"That's very kind, Manuel."

Before leaving, still on the threshold, the dragoman has one hesitation.

"May I ask you a question, master?"

"But of course."

"What did you do all night in the candlelight? Did you work on the bridge?"

Michelangelo smiles at the translator's naïve curiosity.

"No, at the risk of disappointing you, no. I tackled a much more arduous task, my friend. A real challenge."

The artist senses that the answer does not entirely satisfy his interlocutor, who remains motionless, his hand on the door.

"I drew an elephant," he adds.

Guessing that he won't learn any more, Manuel, bewildered, leaves the room to go to the kitchens.

THE DAY BEFORE YESTERDAY MONKEYS AND ELE-
phants; today iron, silver, brass. In the dazzling heat of the forge,
Mesihi shows Michelangelo the work of the sultan's artisans.
The most perfect balance between hardness and ductility: that's
what gives a dagger or sabre its resistance and sharpness.

It's a rare privilege Mesihi has obtained from Ali Pasha for
the Florentine. The arsenal and its techniques are guarded
even more jealously than the harem. Set a little apart from the
city, to prevent fires, the arsenal forges swords, armor, culverin
cannons, and arquebuses. In the heart of this arsenal, a small
workshop produces the most beautiful blades using ingots of
indestructible steel imported from India, in which the concen-
tric outlines of the damask steel are already visible.

Michelangelo is fascinated by the smiths' activities, by the
power of the forgers and bellows handlers. The head of the workshop Michelangelo and Mesihi are visiting is a Syrian, whom the
Sultan captured from the Mamelukes as war booty; he doesn't
seem at all put out by the heat, nor does he seem to perspire,
whereas the artist is swimming in sweat beneath his doublet.

Michelangelo took out of his shirt the drawing he made that
morning, after his night of elephants; it's an ornate dagger with
a straight blade, symmetrical on the axis of the handle, in perfect proportion, according to the golden ratio. The Syrian looks

shocked, tells Mesihi it's impossible to make such a thing, a pagan weapon, in the shape of a Latin cross, it brings misfortune by irritating God; Mesihi of Prishtina smiles, and explains to the Florentine that the drawing is not suitable. Michelangelo is surprised. Still, it is a pure form. Not caring to waste time in theological quibbling, the sculptor asks for an hour, a table, some graphite and red ink for the designs; they set him up in a well-ventilated room off to the side, where the heat is more bearable.

Mesihi doesn't take his eyes off him.

He watches the artist's hand reproduce his initial drawing, finding the proportions with a compass; then slightly curving the blade downward, starting from the second third, a curve he compensates for by a bend in the upper part of the handle, which gives the whole an imperceptibly snakelike movement, an undulation he will hide with a simple border, supported by the lower section. Two curves that complete and annul each other in the violence of the point.

The Latin cross has disappeared and given way to a masterpiece of innovation and beauty.

A miracle.

He had asked for an hour and, in forty minutes, the two sketches are finished, front and back, as well as a medallion for the detail of the handle.

Pleased with himself, Michelangelo smiles; he asks for a little water, which Mesihi hurries to procure for him before running to show this beauty to the Syrian, who is amazed in turn.

Then they have to choose the type of damask steel; Michelangelo decides on one of the most solid kinds, quite dark, whose almost invisible lines won't disturb the design.

It will be a king's weapon.

The wealthy Aldobrandini will have to pay a royal price for it.

Happy, the two artists return to their boat and leave Scutari for Stambul.

Sailing on the calm waters of the Bosphorus, Michelangelo remembers the crossing that separates Mestre from Venice, which he visited in his youth; it is not surprising that there are so many Venetians here, he thinks. This city resembles La Serenissima, but in fabulous proportions, where everything's multiplied by a hundred. A Venice invaded by the seven hills and the power of Rome.

Constantinople, May 23, 1506
  To Buonarroto di Lodovico di Buonarrota Simoni in Firenze

  Buonarroto, you can tell Aldobrandini that I'll have his dagger, and it will be splendid. I think I can send it to him by the beginning of next month. It might be safer to wait for my return so that I can bring it myself, but he'll have to be patient for a little while longer. I don't see my work advancing here and so I can't yet settle on a date.

  I read in your letter that you're getting along perfectly and I'm happy to hear it.

  As for the sum you ask of me again, I understand your needs; know that here my poor room is costing me a fortune and that I haven't yet received the promised payments. As I told you, I beg you to rely on the Santa Maria Maggiore account if Giovan Simone insists.

  Pray God that everything goes for the best.
  Nothing else.

  Your Michelagnolo

ON MAY 27, THE GRAND VIZIER ALI PASHA SUMMONS Michelangelo by way of Mesihi. He wants to find out how the work is advancing. The poet is a little nervous as he transmits this request to the Florentine; he sensed impatience in the Vizier's order, an impatience that stems no doubt from the Sultan himself.

Bayezid is worried about his bridge.

The ceremony is less impressive than during their first meeting. Ali Pasha receives the sculptor after a meeting with his council, the *divan*; Michelangelo had to wait a long time, seated in the shade of a tree, accompanied by Mesihi the functionary who had found it difficult to conceal his anxiety and kept pacing back and forth like the monkey in its cage.

Falachi came to fetch Michelangelo and his companion to bring them to the deputy of the Shadow of God on Earth. The Genoese is less gracious than usual, and Michelangelo begins to feel the tension that is already agitating his companion.

Seated on a platform, surrounded by ministers and servants, Ali Pasha waves to Mesihi to approach. Michelangelo remains respectfully behind.

The dialogue is brief; the Vizier utters a few scant sentences to which his protégé replies with a word.

Then it's the Florentine's turn.

This time the Vizier speaks Turkish. Falachi translates.

"The Sultan is impatient to see your drafts, Maestro. We are too."

"This will soon be possible, my Lord. In ten days at most."

"We have been told that you have not used the engineers and draftsmen at your disposal, and that you haven't been using the workshop we opened for you. Why? Is it not to your liking?"

"Yes, my Lord, of course it is. It's just too soon. As soon as I have some drafts ready, I'll have the models made and will carry out the designs."

"That is good. We will wait for your results, then. Go back to work, and God be with you."

Michelangelo senses this phrase signifies his dismissal; he bows respectfully and Falachi takes him by the arm to lead him away. Still standing, they wait for a few seconds for Ali Pasha to give a final recommendation to Mesihi, a piece of advice that makes the page smile; if Michelangelo had understood Turkish, he'd have heard that the Vizier hoped his protégé hadn't converted the architect invited by the Sultan to his own debauched habits, and that the delay in his work wasn't because of too many visits to the tavern.

Leaving the interview, stepping through the door from the council leading to the courtyard, Michelangelo is in a bad mood.

Under every sky, then, one must humiliate oneself before the powerful.

No more money.

No more purse of aspers to cover his expenses.

Not a penny of what had been outlined in the contract.

Should one be led to believe that wealth and pomp call for stinginess?

In the lingua franca they've worked out during their meetings, Michelangelo opens up to Mesihi, who is a little annoyed by the artist's remark. No, Ali Pasha and Bayezid are neither miserly nor ungrateful. The sculptor has only to show him a single drawing and he'll be showered in gold.

He could even be received by the Sultan in person, a very rare privilege for a foreigner.

On the square where the monumental entrance to the new palace stands, there is a large gathering and many drums; a herald is shouting; a troop of Janissaries is parting the crowd.

"It's an execution, Maestro. Let's go on our way."

But Michelangelo wants to see. He who learned anatomy by dissecting rotting corpses in the morgues of Florence, who saw Savonarola die on the stake, is frightened neither by blood nor by violence to the body. He approaches, followed reluctantly by Mesihi.

"This isn't a spectacle for you to see, Maestro. Let's go."

Michelangelo insists. He takes his place in the audience, in the front.

The pale condemned man is dragged by his chains; the jailers gently get him to kneel. The man lets himself be manipulated, he seems already to be elsewhere; he bows down on his own, presenting his neck.

The executioner approaches, the blade of his sabre shines for an instant in the sun. The crowd's absolute silence lets the brief crack of the vertebrae be heard, the ripping of flesh, the dull thud of the head on the pavement and the fluid lapping of blood gushing onto the ground.

Michelangelo closes his eyes for a second to commend the poor man's soul to God.

The executioner's assistants gather up the remains with respect and wrap them in linen.

Mesihi has turned his eyes away in disgust.

Michelangelo is surprised by the condemned man's docility.

"They probably gave him some opium to relieve his suffering. Let's go, now."

The sculptor, persuaded now that there's nothing more to see, follows his guide.

"Mesihi?"

"Yes, Maestro?"

"Stop calling me *Maestro,* please. My friends call me Michelangelo."

The poet, flattered and moved, quickly resumes walking so he won't be seen blushing.

IN ONE OF THE PENDENTIVES IN THE SISTINE CHAPEL, opposite the panel on which Judith is majestically carrying the head of Holofernes, David is getting ready to decapitate Goliath; his arm, in pure blue pigment, wields a broad scimitar parallel to the ground; a spot of light falls on his shoulder, twisted from the effort.

Of course, Michelangelo is not now thinking of these frescoes, which he will bring into being three years from now, and which will earn him even more measureless glory; right now, he just has a bridge in mind, a bridge whose design he wants to finish as promptly as possible so he can receive his wages and leave this disturbing city, at once familiar and resolutely other, through which he nevertheless doesn't get tired of strolling and gathering images, faces, and colors.

Michelangelo works—that is, he draws in the morning, as soon as the dawn light permits him; then Manuel comes to read to him and he dozes off a little. Toward evening, he walks with Mesihi, whose company he appreciates as much as his beauty. He leaves him before nightfall, when the poet invariably goes to the tavern to get drunk until dawn.

Michelangelo was not very handsome, with a forehead that was too broad, a crooked nose—broken during a brawl in his youth—bushy eyebrows, ears that stuck out a little. He couldn't stand his own face, it was said. It was often said that if he sought perfection of features, beauty in faces, it's because he himself lacked them completely. Only old age and fame would give him an unparalleled aura, like a kind of patina on an object that started out ugly. Perhaps it's in this frustration that we can find the energy of his art; in the violence of the era, in the humiliation of artists, in rebellion against nature, in the lure of money, the inextinguishable thirst for advancement and glory that is the most powerful of motivators.

Michelangelo is searching for love.

Michelangelo is afraid of love just as he's afraid of Hell.

He looks away when he feels Mesihi's gaze resting on him.

MICHELANGELO IS SCREAMING. IT'S THE SEVENTH time he's been tortured. They press a red-hot iron to his legs; the pain keeps him from smelling the stench of burnt flesh. With a pair of tongs, they tear off part of his breast, some shreds of skin from his thighs and shoulders; they break his left arm with a hammer. He faints.

They revive him by throwing buckets of ice water on him.

He moans.

He implores God and his torturers.

He wants to die; they won't let him die; the Inquisitor pours acid on his wounds, he screams again, his body is nothing but one immense spasm, a stretched bow of suffering.

He can no longer even manage to groan, he is blind, everything is dark, painful, buzzing.

The next day they carry him to the stake, to a square brimming with people, people full of hatred, happy to watch the execution, shouting encouragements to the executioner.

He is overcome with fear, the panic fear of suffering and death when he approaches the pyre and he can hear the flames crackling beneath him, he is going to burn, he is burning, the noise of the blaze covers his desperate screams.

He wakes up in a sweat, his mouth dry, just before his ashes are thrown into the Arno.

It's been a long time since he's dreamt of Savonarola. Almost two years. The preacher's death catches up with him sometimes, his face dilated by heat into an immense inaudible cry, his boiling eyes exploding, his outstretched hands where the bones show beneath the skin.

Michelangelo shivers; he stares into the night and breathes in desperately, as if to swallow the light.

ON MAY 30, WHILE HIS WORK IS NOT MAKING ANY progress—he isn't happy with any of the numerous sketches he has drawn—Michelangelo receives a letter that had come from Italy along with Maringhi's goods. He is surprised it's not from his brothers; he does not recognize the beautiful handwriting—wide and authoritative—spread out over two pages.

He trembles as he reads. He turns pale. He stamps his foot. He turns the letter over in every direction, turns red with anger, furiously crumples the missive into a ball, then unfolds it, rereads it; his terrible cry of rage alerts the dragoman Manuel, who arrives in time to see him tearing the letter up and sending all the things on his table flying with a sweep of his arm—ink, quill, charcoal, papers.

Manuel prefers to run discreetly away when confronted by the artist's fury.

The monkey hides under the bed, terrified.

So there it is.

Some good soul has let Rome know of his presence near the Grand Turk. What had to happen has happened. They threaten to inform the Pope, they predict his ruin, excommunication, death even, if he does not return to the fold.

This missive does not, however, come from the Holy Father. It is not signed. He should know that the Sublime Porte is at peace with the Italian states for now. The great empire is powerful. Michelangelo was hired honestly, as he could have been in Milan or France. Even Leonardo worked for the Sultan. This is a new cabal. He pictures the envious people still trying to destroy him, to humiliate him by keeping him from completing the great work that is waiting for him in Constantinople and that will earn him an ever more immense fame, throughout the whole world this time.

They don't want him to succeed. They want him to remain a little court sculptor, a servant, forever.

He sees clearly which jealous architect could be behind this note.

In the evening, when he joins Mesihi for their stroll, Michelangelo has calmed down a little; anger has given way to melancholy, which twilight over the Bosphorus and the long plaint of the muezzin do nothing to appease, quite the contrary. Mesihi had heard of that afternoon's episode from Manuel, but he does not mention it. He notices that his companion suddenly seems tired, that he is even quieter than usual.

They stroll through the city; Michelangelo is slightly stooped, drags his feet a little; his gaze, usually lively and curious, is fixed on the ground in front of him.

Mesihi does not question him.

Mesihi is discreet.

He is content to walk a little closer to the sculptor than usual, almost touching him, so he can feel the presence of a friendly body.

They head west, where the sun has disappeared, leaving a pink trail above the hills; they pass the grandiose mosque that Bayezid has just finished, surrounded by schools and caravanserais; they follow the crest a little, then go downhill before reaching the aqueduct built by some forgotten Caesar which bisects the city with its red-brick arches. There is a little square there, in front of an old church dedicated to Saint Thomas; the view is magnificent. The fires on the Pera towers are lit; the Golden Horn is lost in the meanderings of dark fog and, to the east, the Bosphorus outlines a grey barrier dominated by the somber shoulders of Santa Sophia, guardian of the gap that separates them from Asia.

Michelangelo is thinking of Rome.

He observes this foreign city, Byzantium lost to Christianity; he feels alone, more alone than ever before, guilty, destitute. In his mind he goes over the words and threats in the mysterious letter.

Mesihi takes him gently by the arm.

"Is everything all right, Maestro?"

It annoys him to be treated like an old man or a woman, and he violently repels the poet's hand.

How could he have come here? Why hadn't he been content to send a drawing, like that oaf Leonardo?

If Michelangelo hadn't turned his head away, Mesihi could have seen tears of anger shining in his eyes.

Now he has to make a decision.

He can't risk everything he has built up till now—his career, his genius, his reputation—for a Sultan who hasn't even deigned to meet him.

He stood up to Julius II, that warrior Pope; he can easily stand his ground with Bayezid. But he hasn't yet drawn the bridge. He still hasn't had the idea he's lacking. So he can't claim his wages; to leave now would be not only to lose face, but also the wealth the Sultan is offering him.

This unexpected wrinkle haunts him.

Mesihi is patient; he remains silent for a few minutes, for Michelangelo to pull himself together, then he says quietly: "Look over there, Maestro."

Surprised, the sculptor turns around.

"Look there, down below."

Michelangelo glances over the landscape disappearing into the night, without making anything out but the lights of the towers and a few reflections on the water.

"You will add beauty to the world," Mesihi says. "There is nothing more majestic than a bridge. No poem or story can ever have that strength. When they speak of Constantinople, they'll mention Santa Sophia, Bayezid's mosque, and your work, Maestro. Nothing else." Flattered and touched, Michelangelo smiles as he watches the beacons guide the boats in their dance over the black waves.

MAYBE IT'S BECAUSE HE'S WORRIED AND OPPRESSED that Michelangelo agrees to follow the man from Prishtina to the tavern that night; maybe also because of the trust he has in that miscreant poet whose verses he doesn't know. Maybe simply the spirit of this place won out over his austerity. So he follows close behind a Mesihi who's disconcerted by his decision, contrary to their habits. Since the Turk would be ashamed to take the artist to one of those soldiers' dives he's fond of in the Tahtakale neighborhood, he decides to cross the city and go to one of the many taverns on the other side of the Golden Horn.

On the harbor they easily find a ferryman and, after a brief crossing, they hurry under the Saint Claire gate, just before it closes for the night; the drinkers won't be able to leave the neighborhood before dawn.

Michelangelo already regrets his sudden decision; he'd have done better to go back to his room and continue his drawings, but the strange threatening letter has acted like an energizing wine once the shock and anger passed. He is not one to let himself be intimidated, not at all.

This isn't the first time some jealous individual has sought to harm him.

Upon reflection, the fact that they know he's with the Grand Turk no longer really worries him.

Bayezid is the prince of a great European power, for now at peace with the cities of Italy. A pox on anyone who finds fault with that.

You have to be able to follow something to the end.

Mesihi is delighted at finding his companion smiling again; he projects his own desires onto the Florentine and attributes this change in mood to the prospect of drink. This improvised evening must be perfect. They have to eat, so as not to drink on an empty stomach, so they sit down at an inn where they are served a few slices of a roll of spiced tripe which they eat with noodle soup. The district's population surprises Michelangelo again: Turks, Latins, Greeks, and Jews, from the Gate of Saint Anthony to the Gate of the Bombardes. Jews and Christians are free to settle wherever they like, the only restriction being that they can neither live nor build a place of worship near a mosque. Pera is not a ghetto. It is an extension of Constantinople.

The two men walk past the swollen bastion of the former Genoese Galata Tower, beyond which the cemeteries stretch out; Michelangelo is surprised that, without any apparent danger, one can stroll on foot through the city at night. He thinks about his bridge, about that thread that will join these northern neighborhoods with the center of the capital. What a fabulous city will be born then. One of the most powerful in the world, without a doubt.

He had come for the money, to surpass Leonardo and avenge himself on Pope Julius II, and now the task is transforming him, just as the *Pietà* or *David* transformed him. Michelangelo is shaped by his work.

They walk southward down a slight slope. Mesihi has decided where he'll take the sculptor; his steps quicken. He remembers Michelangelo's emotion last week, faced with dance and music.

Around the former Italian church of San Domenico, which was transformed into a mosque a dozen years ago, is the Andalusian quarter, where those expelled from Grenada have settled; the Sultan chased the Dominicans out of their convent to offer it to the refugees, in compensation for the brutality of the Catholic Kings.

At a respectful distance from the religious building a nameless tavern is hidden, a low door in an old Genoese house, from which the fervor of melancholy oozes.

Mesihi is recognized as soon as they come in. Several drinking companions stand to greet him; they bow to him as before a great personage. The room, its walls decorated with multicolored ceramics all the way down to a good meter from the floor, is strewn with deep cushions and scattered with oil lamps filling the atmosphere with smoke. They guess Michelangelo is a foreigner, from his high doublet and surcoat; a foreigner or a Frank from the neighborhood no one recognizes yet. They are seated in a comfortable corner and brought a little table with a copper tray, some tumblers and a pitcher. The Florentine thinks these people handle the drinking business well; he watches the guests alternating glasses of wine with scented water, which they sometimes mix together; cupbearers weave between the groups, elegantly pouring the thick fluid. The beverage is sweet, with a taste of herbs; the first two glasses are drunk quickly, to reach a state one will prolong by slowing down the rhythm.

After the second glass, Michelangelo is perfectly relaxed.

He observes the designs on the faience tiles, the faces in the shadows, the movements of the servants; he listens to the Andalusian Arab's rough melody, which he is hearing for the first time, mingling with the singsong accents of the Turk.

He who doesn't frequent cheap Florentine restaurants, even less the Roman dives, feels strangely at ease in this ambiance that is neither overly wild nor too refined, far from the excesses of languor or splendor usually attributed to the Orient.

Mesihi too seems happy; he is in deep conversation with one of his neighbors, a young man with a handsome face, dressed in the Turkish style with a dark kaftan and light-colored shirt, who came in not long after they did; from the gazes directed at him, Michelangelo understands they're talking about him, and in fact, soon after, Mesihi introduces them to each other.

The young man's name is Arslan; he has lived for a long time in Venice, and, to the artist's great surprise, not only does he speak a perfect Italian, tinged with Venetian, but he has also seen in the square outside the Palazzo della Signoria the *David* that has earned the sculptor so much glory.

"It's a joy to see two artists like you together," says Arslan.

Mesihi is perhaps even more flattered than Michelangelo.

"Let us drink in honor of this meeting, which cannot be by chance. I've just arrived from Italy, where I went with some merchants; this is my first evening in the city. I haven't seen the capital for two years, and it's a happy omen to find you here."

So they drink.

Then come music and song; Michelangelo has the immense surprise of seeing the same singer from the week before, who walks into the middle of the circle of guests, accompanied by a lute and a tambourine with cymbals, and intones a *muwashshah*, about the lost gardens of Andalusia, flowers, and a fine rain of love and spring. Michelangelo turns slowly to Mesihi and smiles at him; he guesses his friend has prepared this surprise for him and has led him on purpose to the tavern where the fashionable singer was performing.

Michelangelo is again fascinated by the singer's grace, by the sad joy of the melody; he listens with only a distracted ear to Arslan's explanations. This time, he is convinced it's a woman, because of a slight swelling of the chest, visible when she breathes.

The guessing game amuses him just as her beauty seduces him, despite the strangeness of this unknown music.

What's more, it seems to him that the singer is directing complicit glances at him, perhaps because she has recognized him, the only guest dressed in the Frankish style.

The audience is moved to tears; it is overwhelmed by the memory of that vanished land, with its box hedges, the softness of its snow.

Since he has no idea what the kingdom of Grenada could have been, or its fall, or the violence of the Catholic Kings, Michelangelo interprets this fervor as an excess of feeling.

THE FIVE SILVER ANKLETS AROUND THE SLIM LEG, the dress with its orangey tints, the golden shoulder and the beauty spot at the base of the neck will show up in a corner of the Sistine chapel a few years later. In painting as in architecture, the work of Michelangelo Buonarroti will owe much to Istanbul. His gaze is transformed by the city and otherness: scenes, colors, forms will permeate his work for the rest of his life. The cupola of St. Peter is inspired by Santa Sophia and Bayezid's mosque; the library of the Medicis is inspired by the Sultan's, which he visits with Manuel; the statues in the chapel of the Medicis and even the *Moses* for Julius II bear the imprint of attitudes and characters he met here, in Constantinople.

Unlike last week, when too many emotions intermingled with wine put him to sleep like a child in the presence of Ali Pasha, tonight the alcohol renders his perceptions more powerful and increases his pleasure.

He would like to know this singer, male or female.

He who has always put desire off till later, who sees love as a divine song separated from the flesh, something that has passed into poetry like the arm's movement into marble, for eternity, he trembles to approach this moving form, perfect, other, un-defined.

Mesihi and Arslan note his confusion; the former is a little jealous, the other amused. The singers and cupbearers are there to charm and seduce.

Arslan says a few words to Mesihi in a low voice; the poet seems to hesitate an instant, distressed, but appears to adjust to the young man's ideas, even though he barely knows him.

Arslan offers to continue their evening at his place, a stone's throw away, and to invite the beautiful Andalusian woman (if she is indeed a woman, and if she is Andalusian) to sing and dance for them alone, in honor of the great Florentine artist.

When they reveal the idea to Michelangelo, he is delighted. So they drink one final glass as they wait for the end of the song; the tavern is crowded, noisy, smelly; the sculptor lets himself give in to the sweet derangement of all his senses. Never has he been so far from Florence and his brothers, so far from Rome, the Pope, the conspiracies of Raphael and Bramante, so far from his art.

Arslan has discreetly made arrangements to organize the continuation of the evening's entertainment by sending someone to warn his servants, so that supper can await them; then, just as discreetly, he engaged the singer through the tavern keeper and settled their bill of five *akçe* with resounding, tumbling silver pieces.

Mesihi is mistrustful; a shadow of jealousy, true; nevertheless, the unusual prodigality of this stranger is suspicious.

Arslan's amiability to the sculptor borders on obsequiousness.

MESIHI HAS SUFFERED FROM YIELDING THE OBJECT of his love to other embraces, abandoning it to other gazes; this subtle and original poet, master in the rebirth of Ottoman poetry, whose verses will inspire hundreds of imitators, sacrifices his passion in mournful generosity. He who has possessed the bodies and hearts of the most elegant beauties in the city, who has described them in a versified catalogue worthy of Don Giovanni's, full of tenderness and humor, has set his own happiness after the artist's.

Michelangelo smells as bad as a barbarian or a slave from the North who's just been captured; his face is unsightly, far from the ephebes of Shiraz with their Indian beauty spots; his voice is full of anger and without refinement, his hands hard, worn by the chisel and hammer of his art; but despite everything, despite it all, his force, his intelligence, his brute perseverance, the keen song you can guess in his passionate soul, all of these things hopelessly attract Mesihi — but the sculptor doesn't seem to notice.

Downstairs, in the large room scantily illuminated by iron candelabras, the poet sits, glass in hand, exchanging every now and then a few unremarkable phrases with an amused Arslan, but dares not imagine what is happening upstairs, where Michelangelo wanted to go rest, joined immediately, at a sign from their host, by the Andalusian singer.

The night is well advanced, but it still has two or three hours left before it dies; already dark lines are surrounding Mesihi's eyes. He can't help but be angry at this Arslan who has appeared like a djinn in a fairy tale to take him away, with his machinations, from this disheveled Frank whom he desires so strongly.

He begins to recite some verses.

A Persian poem.

> *I don't stop desiring when my desire*
> *Is fulfilled, when my mouth wins*
> *The red lips of my beloved,*
> *When my soul expires in the sweetness of her breath.*

Arslan smiles, he has recognized the inimitable Hafez of Shiraz, which is confirmed by the last couplet:

> *And you will always invoke the name of Hafez*
> *In the company of the sad and the brokenhearted.*

ALMOST COMPLETE DARKNESS.

Only a candle outside the room casts a little light through the half-open door.

Michelangelo guesses, more than sees, the contours of that slender body, lithe and muscular, that lets its clothes slip to the floor.

He hears its bracelets tinkling when the dark shape approaches him, preceded by a perfume of musk and rose and warm sweat.

The sculptor turns over, huddles at the edge of the bed.

She sang for him, this shadow, and now here she is next to him, and he does not know what to do; he is ashamed and very afraid; she stretches out against him, to touch him; when he feels her breath he shivers, as if the night wind, come from the sea, suddenly chilled him.

A hand rests on his upper arm; he stops trembling; this caress is burning.

He doesn't know which of their two pulses he feels beating so strongly through these fingers.

A warm wave of hair travels over the back of his neck.

Eyes closed, he imagines the young man or woman behind him, elbow bent, face above his own.

He remains motionless, rigid as a pointer.

FINALLY I'M GOING TO TELL YOU A STORY. YOU HAVE nowhere to go. The night is all around you, you are locked up in a remote fortress, prisoner of my caresses; you do not want my body, fine, but you can't escape my voice. It's the very ancient story of a country that today has disappeared. Of a forgotten country, a Sultan who was a poet and a Vizier, his lover.

There was war, not just between Muslims, but also against the Christians. They were powerful. The Prince lost battles, he had to leave Córdoba, abandon Toledo; his enemies were everywhere. His Vizier had been his tutor; now he was his confidant, his lover. For a long time, they improvised poems together in gardens, by fountains; they got drunk on beauty. One time, the Vizier saved the city by suggesting to the King of the Franks that he play chess for the city: if he won, they'd give him the keys, if he lost, the siege would be lifted. They used beautiful jade chessmen, from the other side of the world. The Vizier ended up winning and the Christian King left for the north, taking the chess board away as his sole booty.

One day, as the Prince and the Vizier were enjoying themselves by the river, a young female servant delighted them with her witty repartees, her immense beauty, the refinement of her culture and her poetry. The Sultan fell madly in love with her and took her off to his palace. The former slave he turned into his queen.

She was so beautiful and so refined that the Prince turned completely away from his minister, whom he now consulted only for affairs of state. The Vizier suffered; he mourned the loss of the Sultan's attentions, and at the same time burned with a secret love for the inaccessible wife of his King.

He went away, of his own volition, appointing himself governor of a remote fortress.

The sadness of lost pleasures, the memory of the time of poems and songs, joined in his heart with the terrible desire to possess the beautiful princess, out of revenge, out of love.

Desperate, he decided to join forces with the Christians to seize hold of the capital and make the sublime slave his own.

He committed treason without remorse.

He placed his armies at the service of the Franks.

Together they laid siege to the city.

The Sultan, crushed by his friend's defection, locked himself up in his room without resolving to fight. He composed a poem, which he himself set forth in calligraphy and sent via messenger to the rebel Vizier.

The shadow of pleasure is always above me:
This cloud of absence weeps the wine that intoxicates me.
For me your weapons strike the sweet blows of love,
I give you this kingdom, so that you cannot lose it.

Moved to tears by this declaration, the Vizier decided to betray a second time; he turned his army against the Christians by surprise and, after a bitter battle, entered the city as conqueror.

He set down his weapons in front of the Prince as a sign of submission.

The Sultan invited him to his room that very night.

He took the Vizier in his arms tenderly, then, without hesitation, he drew out his sword and ripped him open from shoulder to chest.

The Vizier expired on the floor; he did not hear his friend's words:

> *You did not know how to rise to the height of love*
> *And like the falcon take what was within your reach*
> *The prey was yours, you let it go*
> *Lovers are cruel if they see the beloved weaken.*
> *This battle I have won, I lose.*
> *This ground I defend will be my wilderness,*
> *And the souls of those I have slain,*
> *My wardens for eternity.*

You have listened to this story? It is true, take care. You refuse my caresses. I could have a sword too. I could slice you in half for your scorn. I am here and you reject me. You're sleeping, who knows. You're breathing gently. The night is long. You don't understand me, perhaps. You let yourself be lulled to sleep by the accents of my voice. You feel as if you're elsewhere. You are not far away, though. Not very far from your home. You are where I am, you know it. You will come there; perhaps someday you will face the fact of love like the Vizier. You will give your passion free rein. Make up your mind, like the bird of prey. Make up your mind to join me among these dead stories.

MICHELANGELO WILL NOT TALK ABOUT THIS NIGHT in the quiet of the bedchamber beyond the fresh water of the Golden Horn, not to Mesihi, not to Arslan, even less to his brothers or, later on, to the few lovers he is known to have had; he keeps this memory somewhere in his painting and in the secret of his poetry: his sonnets are the only uncertain trace of what has vanished forever.

As for Mesihi, he will express his suffering more clearly; he will compose two ghazals on the burning of jealousy, a sweet burning, for it fortifies love by consuming it.

He spent the night drinking, alone when their host withdrew in turn, conquered by fatigue; he saw the Andalusian beauty discreetly leave the house at dawn, wrapped in a long cloak; he patiently waited for Michelangelo, who avoided his gaze; he took the exhausted sculptor to the steam baths, convinced his torn-apart soul to submit to his hands; he bathed him, massaged him, rubbed him fraternally; he left him to doze off on a warm marble bench, wrapped in white linen, and watched over him as he would a corpse.

When Michelangelo emerges from his torpor and shakes himself, Mesihi is still by his side.

The sculptor is full of dazzling energy, despite the alcohol ingested the night before and the lack of sleep, as if by ridding himself of encrustations and filth he had gotten rid of the weight of remorse or overindulgence; he thanks the poet for his care and asks him to be kind enough to accompany him back to his room, for he wants to get back to work.

As they cross the Golden Horn, Michelangelo has a vision of his bridge, floating in the morning sun, so real that he has tears in his eyes. The edifice will be colossal but not imposing: delicate and powerful. As if the evening had opened his eyes and transmitted its certainty, the drawing finally appears to him.

He returns almost at a run to set this idea down on paper, lines in ink, shadows in white, highlights in red.

A bridge that has risen up out of the night, molded from the material of the city.

Buonarroto,

I received your letter and I understand you. Forgive my not writing more, know that I'm overwhelmed with work. I am going to work day and night to finish my labors and join you as soon as possible.

I'm thinking of Giovan Simone and the money, soon I'll find some arrangement, if God gives me life.

For now you can go see Aldobrandini and ask him for an advance on the price of the dagger. He will not be disappointed. Never has anyone seen such a fine one, I swear it.

Pray for me,

Your Michelagnolo

FOUR LOW ARCHES SUPPORT AN ARC WITH SUCH A gentle curve that it's almost imperceptible; they rest on sturdy pillars whose triangular cutwaters cleave the water like bastions. Supported by an invisible foundation that barely reaches above the waves, a majestic footbridge gently joins the two shores, reconciling their differences. Two hands placed majestically on the waters, two slender fingers that touch each other.

The Grand Vizier Ali Pasha is astonished.

Bayezid will be delighted.

Michelangelo has submitted his sketches and drawings to the model-makers and engineers; he has supervised the realization of scale models and large plans to present to the Sultan. As a remarkable honor, the sculptor is invited to reveal his work himself to the sovereign. The question of the buttress and the road traffic has yet to be resolved, matters that regard the *shehremini* and the *mohendesbashi*.

The Florentine has fulfilled his contract: he has projected a bridge over the Golden Horn, bold and political; far from Da Vinci's technical prowess, far from the regular curves of Constantine's old viaduct, beyond the classics. All his energy can be found in it. This work is like *David*; his strength and calm can be read in it, along with the possibility of a storm. Solemn and graceful at the same time.

The day before the presentation to the Sultan, Mesihi and Michelangelo went to the Scutari arsenal to pick up the dagger ordered by the wealthy Florentine Aldobrandini; sharpened and polished, in a box lined with red flannel, the black damask steel is extraordinarily beautiful. Caressing the blade with his finger, the sculptor thinks it will be hard for him to give it away when the time comes.

Absorbed by his work, Michelangelo hasn't thought much about the night spent at the home of the obliging Arslan; Mesihi hasn't mentioned it either, for other reasons. He feels his passion for the artist devouring his heart; during their daily strolls, in the evening, when the cool breezes rise from the Bosphorus to fill the city, he profits from the walk to hold his friend's arm at times and, once he has dropped him off at Maringhi's, he invariably goes to the tavern, where he drowns his sadness in wine until dawn. His relations with the Vizier, his employer, are strained; he is blamed for his absences; often, when Ali Pasha sends for him to write a letter or inscribe a firman in calligraphy, he can't be found, and then all the dives in Tahtakale have to be searched to unearth him.

Mesihi senses that Michelangelo does not look at him with the same warmth that Mesihi feels for the Florentine; Michelangelo is sometimes harsh, cold even, with a harshness and coldness that only sharpen the poet's passion even more, and he would pay dearly for one night with the artist, like the Andalusian beauty. But he respects the distance there is between them. He also respects Michelangelo's sobriety and his passion for work, whose wonderful results he has just discovered, at the same time as the Vizier.

Tomorrow, the models and drawings will be brought before the Sultan. To prevent any public disappointment, Ali Pasha has already shown a drawing to the sovereign in secret, and has been assured of his agreement. The ceremony planned for the next day will be a confirmation.

Michelangelo is eager to receive his earnings and get back to Florence.

To Maestro Giuliano da Sangallo, architect to the Pope in Rome

Giuliano, as a sign of my friendship I'm sending you these cross-sections and elevations of the Santa Sophia Basilica in Constantinople, which I received from a Florentine merchant by the name of Maringhi; they are extraordinary. I hope you will profit from them.

I ask you again, my dearest Giuliano, to send me His Holiness' reply about the tomb.

Nothing more.

This day June 6, 1506,
Your Michelagnolo, sculptor in Florence.

MICHELANGELO IS DAZZLED BY THE OPULENCE AND splendor of the court. The crowd of slaves, ministers, the highest-ranking janissaries, the noble, serene look of the Sultan wearing a white turban adorned by a golden aigrette with diamonds — all these fascinate him. Bayezid's architects have built the model in just three days, and it now sits enthroned on a rich display stand, which irritates the artist; the model is six cubits long and one and a half high. He would have preferred it to be shown on a simple table, but the rules of etiquette demand that only noble objects may be presented to the sovereign.

Bayezid does not hide his joy.

He displays a wide smile.

He congratulates the sculptor himself, directly, and even goes so far — a rare event — as to thank him in Frankish.

Ambassadors from Venice or from the King of France are not so well received.

Bayezid solemnly gives the order to the *mohendesbashi* to start construction as soon as possible.

Then the Shadow of God on Earth has the Florentine approach and hands him a rolled parchment covered in his *tughra*, his calligraphic seal; Michelangelo respectfully bows.

He is then given permission to leave.

The interview lasted a few minutes at most, but the artist has had time to stare at the Sultan, to note his robust constitution, his aquiline nose, his large, dark eyes, his black eyebrows, the marks of age around his cheekbones; if he didn't hate portraits so much, Michelangelo would set to drawing him immediately, before he forgot the great lord's features.

MICHELANGELO IS FURIOUS, SEETHING; HE BREAKS two phials of ink and a small mirror, unceremoniously sends the monkey flying across the room, then summons Manuel the dragoman who, after translating the parchment offered by the Sultan, had thought it wise to disappear.

"Find me Mesihi," he shouts.

Manuel obeys immediately and returns an hour later in the company of the poet-secretary.

"What is this," the artist asks, pointing to the piece of paper without any preamble, not even greeting the man who would so like to be his friend.

"It is a gift from the Sultan, Maestro. A deed of property. An immense honor. Foreigners are excluded from these kinds of benefits. Aside from you, Michelangelo."

Mesihi is both sad and angry at Michelangelo's rage. How can he not understand that this parchment represents an exceptional homage?

"You're telling me that I am the owner of a village in the middle of nowhere I know nothing about, is that right?"

"In Bosnia, that's right. A village, the lands attached to it, and all their income."

"So those are my wages?"

"No, Maestro, it's a gift. Your wages will be paid once the construction is well underway."

Mesihi is angry with himself for disappointing the object of his passion in such a way; if he could, he'd shower Michelangelo in gold that very instant.

The Florentine sits down and sorrowfully takes his head in hands.

Turk or Roman, the powerful demean us.

God have pity on me.

Michelangelo understands that Bayezid is holding him in his power for as long as he likes.

He looks at Mesihi with hatred, with such hatred that the poet, if he weren't at least as proud as the sculptor, would burst into tears.

IT IS THE SECOND NIGHT. THE FIRE IS PROJECTING its reddish glints onto your shoulder. You are not drunk.

You are a child, fickle and passionate. You have me lying next to you, but you're not taking advantage of it. What are you thinking about? About whom? You have nothing to do with my love. I know who you are.

They told me.

You are a slave of princes, just as I am a slave of innkeepers and procurers.

Maybe you're right. Maybe the best part of childhood is this stubborn rage that makes us destroy the sandcastle if it isn't perfect, if it doesn't measure up to our desires. Maybe your genius blinds you. I am nothing compared to you, that's for sure. You make me tremble. I feel this dark force that will break everything in its way, destroy everything with its certainties.

You didn't come here to know me, you came to build a bridge, for money, for God knows what else, and you'll leave exactly the same, unchanged, you'll return to your destiny. If you don't touch me you will remain the same. You won't have met anyone. Locked up in your world you see nothing but shadows, unfinished shapes, lands to be conquered. Each day pushes you on to the next, a day you don't really know how to inhabit.

I'm not looking for love. I'm looking for consolation. Comfort for all these countries we have lost since we left our mother's womb, which we replace with stories, like greedy children, our eyes wide open to the storyteller.

The truth is that there is nothing but suffering: we try to forget, in the arms of strangers, that we will soon vanish.

Your bridge will remain; maybe it will take on, as time passes, a very different meaning from the one it has today, just as in my vanished country they'll see something quite different from what it actually was, our successors will hang their stories on it, their worlds, their desires. Nothing belongs to us. They will find beauty in terrible battles, courage in men's cowardliness, everything will enter into legend.

You remain silent, I know you don't understand me.

Let me kiss you.

You elude me like a snake.

You are already far away, too far for anyone to reach you.

THE NEXT DAY, WHEN MESIHI ARRIVES FOR THEIR daily stroll, Michelangelo is in an excellent mood. He doesn't know how to apologize for his behavior the day before. He tactfully welcomes the poet, showers him with compliments, invites him up to his room.

"I have something to show you," he says.

Surprised, Mesihi accompanies him.

Once in the artist's apartment, they keep silent. Mesihi, feeling awkward, doesn't know where to sit; he remains standing.

The monkey seems to respect their silence and remains equally motionless and silent in his cage.

Michelangelo is embarrassed; he observes Mesihi, his elegant bearing, his delicate features, his dark, oiled hair.

Suddenly he hands him a piece of paper.

"This is for you," he says, using the formal word for "you."

This sudden, respectful term of address is very sweet to the poet's ears.

"What is it?"

"It's a drawing. A souvenir. An elephant. It brings luck, they say. It can take the place of a monkey for you," he adds, laughing.

Mesihi smiles.

"Thank you, Michelangelo. It is magnificent."

"And this too is for you. I'm giving it to you."

Michelangelo offers him the roll of parchment the Sultan gave him.

"I cannot accept it, it's a gift from Bayezid, Maestro. It's worth a lot of money."

Michelangelo insists, protests, saying he can't do anything with it, and that, surely, it's possible to have Mesihi's name inscribed in place of his own on this deed of land.

Mesihi continues to refuse energetically, smiling.

"I'll keep the elephant, Maestro. That's enough."

Michelangelo makes as if to give in to Mesihi's arguments and then, a few seconds later, as they're getting ready to leave the room, he says very quietly:

"You know, this paper belongs to you as much as it does to me. Without you, I'd never have gotten anywhere."

And he forcefully places the firman in his hand.

Mesihi feels his heart swelling to the point of breaking.

TO OUTWIT BOREDOM, MICHELANGELO DRAWS GLYPHS, moldings, and scotias on pieces of paper already covered in thighs, feet, ankles, and hands.

He waits.

He jots down endless lists in his notebook.

He works a little on the tomb of Julius Della Rovere, the intransigent Pope who ten years earlier, while still a cardinal, led the Vatican troops against Bayezid's janissaries in southern Italy. Michelangelo has met the two enemies, one after the other, and offered the first a mausoleum, the other a bridge.

Every day, Manuel comes to read to him.

Michelangelo loves stories.

He appreciates nothing so much as tales about battles, the machinations of the wonderful gods on top of Olympus, the combats of angels and demons. He hears images in them; he sees a hero bent by the weight of his sword decapitate the Gorgon, a drop of blood rising up from a young deer's wound, Hannibal's elephants bending their knees in the snow.

He writes a few madrigals.

The memory of the Andalusian beauty, of her whispers in the night, of the contact of her hands, comes back to haunt him often.

Several times, he has almost returned to the tavern, or asked Mesihi to accompany him there; but he confusedly senses the Turk's feelings for him and doesn't want to wound him. He likes this strange friendship; despite what his mood swings and fits of anger might lead one to believe, he feels something for Mesihi and, in the most secret part of his soul, where desires burn, no doubt the poet's portrait can be found there, well hidden.

Michelangelo is obscure even to himself.

When he receives a visit from Arslan one morning, as the completion of the opening in the ramparts preliminary to construction has just been announced to him, he is full of joy. Arslan has heard about the start of work on the bridge, he knows the Sultan is proud of his architect, and he has come to congratulate him and offer his regards. The man is friendly. His conversation is pleasant. The whole capital is talking about nothing but this new work, he says. You're going to be the hero of this city, as in Florence.

Michelangelo, a little embarrassed, doesn't know how to approach the subject that interests him.

They sit down in the courtyard, in the shadow of the fig tree.

They talk about Florence, politics, Rome, in the company of the merchant Maringhi, who already knows Arslan; this coincidence seems like an excellent omen to the artist. He tries to find a way to see the object of his passion again.

It's Maringhi who finds it for him.

"Soon it will be St. John's Day, the patron saint of Florence," the trader says. "I'm going to give a party; I'm counting on you to come."

"I know some excellent musicians," Arslan says, turning toward the sculptor.

Michelangelo can't help but blush.

THE WORKSITE FOR THE NEW BRIDGE OVER THE Golden Horn opens officially on June 20, 1506, with the closing of part of the harbor and the building of a platform to handle the thousands of stones needed for the construction. Earlier on, a large area had been prepared at the foot of the ramparts and the Porte della Farina was enlarged. Michelangelo is still waiting for the promised money; as of now, only a purse containing a hundred silver coins for his expenses has arrived, quickly eaten up by the exorbitant prices Maringhi is demanding for rent and furnishings.

Michelangelo is now even more impatient to get back to Italy since his brothers are constantly pressuring him to return and since he knows, after that mysterious missive from Rome, that certain people are eager to destroy him, to make him look like a renegade, possibly, or worse. He is used to conspiracies. The corridors of the pontifical palace swarm with plotters and assassins; his enemies, Raphael and Bramante especially, are powerful.

They promise he'll soon be able to leave.

Michelangelo is afraid that Bayezid and Ali Pasha are too pleased with him to let him go so quickly.

Constantinople is a very sweet prison.

The city is balanced between east and west as he himself is between Bayezid and the Pope, between Mesihi's tenderness and the burning memory of a dazzling singer.

ARSLAN CAME BACK ONCE TO VISIT THE SCULPTOR.

He found him in his room, busy jotting down the list of his latest expenses.

Arslan is surprised by the presence of the monkey gamboling freely outside its open cage, yelping, leaping from the table to the artist's shoulder, then onto the bed and even onto the visitor's lap.

The Turk roughly shoves it away with his foot.

"Where did you find this creature?"

"It's a gift from Mesihi. It comes from India," Michelangelo proudly adds, smiling.

Arslan shrugs.

"It's horrible, it shouts and smells bad. Be careful, it could bite you."

Michelangelo bursts out laughing.

"No, no, up till now it's only bitten Maringhi, who deserves it. I named him Julius, for his bad character. With me he eats out of my hand, look."

He takes a hazelnut out of a little bag and holds it out to the monkey, who approaches and delicately takes the nut in its tiny fingers, with great respect and real nobility.

Michelangelo can't help but laugh again.

"Isn't he distinguished?"

Arslan looks disgusted.

"There is something diabolical in their almost human behavior, Maestro."

"You think? I find it amusing."

Arslan prefers to change the subject.

"Is there any news about your bridge?"

"Yes. The engineers are arguing over the size and height of the pilings. Construction has begun on both shores; soon I'll draw the details of the arches and pillars and will draft the plans with all the dimensions."

"That hasn't been done yet?"

"No, I'm waiting for the engineers' opinion."

"So you'll be with us for quite a while longer, then."

Michelangelo sighs.

"Possibly."

"You don't seem happy about that."

"I confess I miss Italy. My brothers are asking for me, too."

"If I can help you in any way, don't hesitate to ask. What could make your stay more pleasant?"

The sculptor can't help but think of the Andalusian singer, her voice and hands in the night.

"Nothing you haven't done already, thank you. And Mesihi is seeing to my every wish."

"Ah, Mesihi."

There's something like reproach in Arslan's voice.

"He's a charming companion and a pleasant guide."

"A man who loses himself in wine and opium loses his self."

"True. But he is a great poet."

Arslan pauses.

"Have you heard his poetry, Maestro?"

"I know the extracts that have been translated for me. They're as beautiful as our Petrarch."

"If you say so."

Michelangelo is slightly annoyed by the young man's insinuations. As usual, he can't help replying directly:

"Do you have anything against him?"

Arslan doesn't hesitate for a second.

"No, of course not, on the contrary. He is the protégé of the Grand Vizier; a person's importance can be measured by the power of his friends."

Even without being a seasoned courtier, Michelangelo has grasped the perfidy of Arslan's words.

He'd like the monkey to seize the moment and urinate on the merchant's shoes, but the animal has caught hold of the quill on the writing table and is trying — a furry knight clumsily handling a lance too large for him — to hold it upright and draw God knows what on the paper.

Michelangelo bursts out laughing.

"You see? None of this is very important."

Arslan feels obliged to guffaw with him.

"It's all just a matter of monkeying around, if we are to take your horrible animal literally."

Michelangelo remains silent for a while, before whispering:

"It's true. We all ape God in His absence."

ON JUNE 24, FEAST DAY OF ST. JOHN THE BAPTIST, Maringhi's caravanserai is in full celebration. Michelangelo is more or less the guest of honor; a few Genoese and Venetian traders are there, forgetting their rivalry for once; Mesihi is there too, of course, along with Falachi and all the Florentines and Tuscans present in Istanbul. In the morning everyone went to Mass in the Latin church on the other side of the Golden Horn; everyone is thinking that when evening falls in Florence, they'll light fires along the Arno, and this makes them a little melancholy. Michelangelo keeps company with Mesihi, radiating beauty in his embroidered kaftan. The summer has barely begun and yet the heat is already stifling despite the shade in the courtyard, where the banquet tables are set up. Arslan arrives and respectfully greets the host before coming over to Michelangelo and Mesihi. The sculptor notices the poet wince with surprise or displeasure; he seems not to be very fond of his cosmopolitan compatriot.

Michelangelo is disappointed to see that Arslan has come alone; he had secretly been hoping he'd arrive with the eagerly awaited singer; he dares not ask.

Everyone sits down to eat.

Maringhi has done things well. The banquet is copious, unending.

Michelangelo the frugal, bothered by the heat, eats sparingly.

Halfway through the meal, he abandons his fellow guests and withdraws to his room, claiming fatigue — he, the indefatigable.

He rereads a sonnet written the day before, finds it bad and tears it furiously to pieces.

He doesn't go back down to the courtyard until some hours later.

Mesihi has disappeared.

Half the guests remain.

They are playing games and sipping sorbets.

Arslan is still there, which reassures the artist a little. All hope is not lost. Maybe they'll come later. Yes, that's it, without a doubt. The musicians will arrive at night, with the torches.

Michelangelo tastes the sweet cherry soup chilled with snow from Anatolia or the Balkans compressed into large blocks and preserved in the dark, at the bottom of cisterns, covered in straw.

People offer to play a game of cones or tric-trac with him; he refuses. He dislikes games even more than drinking, if that's possible. He sits down next to Arslan, who displays his eternal smile, and asks him how his business is going, a topic of conversation like any other.

"I can't complain. Peace with the Republic is favorable for trade. I should return to Venice soon. I have a warehouse there, not as large as this one, but flourishing all the same."

Michelangelo finds it difficult to believe that this muscular young man is actually a merchant. One could picture him as a swordsman, even a courtier, but surely not behind a counter, even a Venetian one. He wonders what sort of chance brought him close to Maringhi. No doubt both merchants know each other; perhaps they even buy things from each other.

The Florentines present are cheerful, with a nostalgic cheerfulness; their host has had a pile of wood set up in the middle of the fountain in his courtyard, which he will set alight at night, at the risk of setting the whole neighborhood on fire, which doesn't seem to worry him too much. Michelangelo remembers the St. John festivities in the palace of Lorenzo the Magnificent, when he was still an apprentice, and feels a lump rise in his throat. Life has only given him a few pleasant moments until now; years of relentless work, troubles, and humiliations. But the memories of the palace of the Medicis glow in him with a special light. Beyond the excellent training he received there, in Lorenzo's entourage and in court life there was an almost familial security that he often misses, whether it had come from the insouciance of youth, or his thirst to learn, never quenched. There too he often confronted his comrades; he learned how to sweat, to fight, to suffer and work. It was in the harsh gazes of his masters that Michelangelo found his fathers. In their harshness and their rare tenderness.

Day is beginning to fade away; the sky is streaked with pink, a light sea breeze refreshes the caravanserai; they've opened the gates wide to let the air in, which is now travelling through the arcades and tenderly stirring the leaves of the fig tree.

Mesihi comes back, after having been called away urgently by the Vizier. He seems worried. Michelangelo doesn't pay him much mind.

He is relieved.

He has heard the Florentines whispering that the musicians would soon be arriving; they'd light the fire, there would be drinking.

All of a sudden, he can let himself give in to the lightheartedness of the summer evening.

A SAD OMEN: THIS MORNING THE MONKEY DIED. OR maybe during the night; when Michelangelo woke up, he found him lying on the ground, paws folded in, chin tucked under, as if he had been stopped as he ran.

Michelangelo took the tiny hand in his, lifted it, let it fall back.

He picked the animal up; it seemed to have lost all its weight, to weigh nothing now, as if only the energy of life gave it mass.

It was a little thing that death rendered even more fragile.

Michelangelo felt a lump in his throat. He laid the small body out in the cage, which he unhooked and set on the floor.

He didn't want to see it anymore, so he called a servant to get rid of it immediately, hoping that would also erase the strange sadness that was stifling him. He mourned this death like that of a child he'd barely grown to know.

MICHELANGELO DREAMS OF A BANQUET FROM LONG ago, when you could discuss Eros without your speech being slurred by wine, without your elocution being impaired by it, when beauty was only contemplation of beauty, far from these ugly moments prefiguring death, when bodies fought no longer against their fluids, their moods, their desires. He dreams of an ideal banquet, where table companions wouldn't reel from fatigue or alcohol, when all vulgarity would be banished for the sake of art.

He watches the guests turn ugly in pleasure, all of them, except Arslan and Mesihi, who are sizing each other up strangely, with a look of mutual challenge, almost without bringing their cups to their perfect lips.

There's a mystery there that Michelangelo doesn't try to decipher; he thinks vaguely — since he is vain — that it has to do with him, with his person.

As always when he's about to finish a project, he is both happy and sad; happy to have finished and sad that the work isn't as perfect as if God Himself had created it.

How many works of art will there have to be to put beauty into the world? he thinks as he watches the guests get drunk.

The fire dancing in the basin forms faces; they're all terrible monsters from another age, gargoyles of moving shadows. A single orange-tinged flame hypnotizes him: the body of the singer. Her slight movements, her melody rising up into the night, her hand skillfully tapping the drum to general indifference.

Michelangelo feels anxious.

He wants to have the beloved voice near him in the half light. He senses that Mesihi is watching him with a strange concern. Contradictory feelings agitate him.

This time, he carefully kept himself from touching the heavy wine his compatriots are noisily swigging.

OFTEN ONE WISHES FOR THINGS TO REPEAT; YOU want to relive a moment that escaped, return to a gesture that didn't take place or a word that wasn't uttered; you try to find again the sounds that were left in your throat, the caress you didn't dare give, the tightening of the chest that is gone forever.

Lying on his side in the dark, Michelangelo is disturbed by his own coldness, as if beauty always eluded him. There is nothing palpable, nothing attainable in the body, it slips between the hands and disappears like snow or sand; never does one find unity, never does one attain the flame; once separated, the two heaps of clay will never join, they will wander in the dark, guided by the illusion of a star.

Although he loves this skin against his shoulder, the smooth shiver of foreign hair on his neck, its spicy perfume, the magic has stopped working. Pleasure leaves him unmoved.

He would like to be opened up, so the passion inside could be set free.

He would fly away and burn then, like the phoenix.

YOU FEEL AS IF THE END IS APPROACHING, AS IF THIS is the last night. You will have had the chance to stretch out your hand to me, I will have offered myself in vain. That's how it is. It's not me you desire. I am nothing but the reflection of your poet friend, the one who sacrifices himself for your happiness. I do not exist. Maybe you're discovering that now. You will suffer from it later on, of course; you will forget; in vain you will have covered the walls with our faces, our features will vanish little by little. Bridges are beautiful things, so long as they last; everything will perish. You are capable of stretching out a stone footbridge, but you don't know how to let yourself go in the arms that are waiting for you.

Time will solve all that, who knows. Fate, patience, willpower. Nothing of your time here will remain. Traces, clues, an edifice. Like my vanished country, over there, at the other end of the sea. Now it lives only in stories and in the people who tell them. For a long time they will have to talk about lost battles, forgotten kings, vanished animals. About what was, what could have been, so that it can exist again. This border you trace as you turn your back on me, like a line drawn with a stick in the sand, will be erased someday; someday you too will yield to the present, even if only in death.

Someday you will return.

FOR A LONG TIME MICHELANGELO WATCHED THE young woman sleeping beside him. She is a golden shadow; the flickering candle illumines her ankle, her thigh, her hand closed as if clutching sleep itself or something inaccessible; her skin is dark, Michelangelo gently runs his finger over her arm, then back up to the hollow of her shoulder.

He knows nothing of her; he let himself be charmed by that weary voice, then he watched her doze off as the midsummer fire was dying down, revealing the countless stars of the June night.

Three Spanish words are spinning in his head like a melody.

Reyes, batallas, elefantes.
Battaglie, re, elefanti.

He will record them in his notebook, the way a child fiercely guards his treasure of precious pebbles.

MESIHI ACCOMPANIED ARSLAN TO THE GATE OF THE caravanserai. Drunk, the Florentines went to bed; only Maringhi's servants are still bustling around in the courtyard and making the last traces of the banquet disappear.

Mesihi watches the fire die down little by little, as sadness covers him with its ashes.

He senses he is about to lose Michelangelo forever.

The obsequious Arslan is a strange spy, both an agent from Venice and the Sultan's man; he navigates between each, offering his equivocal services on both sides of the sea.

Here too there are conspiracies and palace intrigue; jealousies, plotters ready to do anything to discredit Ali Pasha in the Bayezid's eyes, to block the construction of this impious bridge, the work of an infidel, to bring about the minister's disgrace by means of a scandal.

Michelangelo suspects nothing.

Mesihi knows that Arslan is a cog in these machinations; he can do nothing against him, even less so because, in exchange for the price of a fief in Bosnia, Arslan has just revealed to him the terms of the conspiracy. Mesihi offered everything he owns for this information.

Now he feels alone and overwhelmed; he knows what he has to do.

He will have to estrange the one he loves in order to protect him.

Tear him away from the deadly Andalusian.

Organize his escape, hide his departure, and bid him farewell.

I'M GOING TO HAVE TO KILL YOU. YOU DON'T KNOW
that. You wouldn't be able to believe it. I am not asleep; I'm
waiting for you to doze off, then I'll take the black dagger on
your table and pass it through your body. There's no point in
being vexed. That's how it is. I have no choice. One always has a
choice. I could give up now; give up the money, face the threats;
if I don't kill you I'll be found drowned on the other side of the
Bosphorus, or strangled in my bedroom with a silken cord. One
can get caught up in dreaming. I could have imagined an escape
into the night, with you or someone else; I have delayed this
moment as long as I could.

I don't know if I'll succeed.

I'll have to muster all the hatred I can feel against your people, and I don't have any. Or not much. I'll have to summon the
strength of the past, imagine I'm avenging my father, my lost
country, my people, scattered, spread out on the shores of the
sea.

I know you have nothing to do with any of that.

Forces pull us, manipulate us in the dark; we resist. I have re-
sisted. Perhaps the last barrier will be fear, the memory of your
hand caressing me gently as if it were discovering the trunk of
an unknown tree.

You do not desire me and yet you are tender.

I won't manage to do it. I don't have the passionate pain of the Vizier betraying his lover; I don't have the jealous anger of the Sultan who kills him.

I have held a weapon one time only, one horrible time, and I trembled from it for a whole year after.

Even soldiers need shouts and the noise of battle to find courage.

I could explain to you why they gave me this task, by what chance; I could tell you about your many enemies, about me, my life, but that would change nothing. Those powerful people you fear have sealed your fate and mine. If you had breathed the madness of love into me, if I had been able to seduce you, perhaps then we could both have saved ourselves.

I tried to love you so I wouldn't have to kill you.

You have fallen asleep.

I'll have to go through with it.

Fortunately in the half light I can barely make out your face; it will be simpler; this blade is so perfect it will slice your throat effortlessly, preventing you from crying out; you'll feel a warm stream flowing down your chest, you'll suffocate without understanding and your strength will leave you.

Judith did it long ago, to save her people. I have no people to save, no old woman to hold a bag in which to hide your head; I am alone and afraid.

This blade is much heavier than a janissary's scimitar; it has the weight of our two lives together.

I'll remain till the end of days with the dagger in my hand, standing in the night, not daring either to leave or to strike you.

MICHELANGELO IS AWAKENED BY A SHOUT, A STRUG-
gle in the dark; he is afraid, rolls to the foot of the bed, without
understanding; a call for help, confused thuds on the floor; he
sees someone bringing a light, he hears his name called.

He gets up with difficulty.

The bloody body of a woman is lying on the ground.

Mesihi is standing, his eyes wild, looking crazed and pale.

He is still brandishing Aldobrandini's black dagger, which
has just penetrated the singer's flesh with such ease.

Michelangelo remains speechless for a few seconds. He can't
look away from the naked body lying on the floor: a black pool
is getting larger under her chest; her face, from the side, half
covered by unkempt hair, is pale as the moon; it seems agitated
by some final movement which is scarcely one, a shiver at most.

On the threshold, the servants with their candles are stupe-
fied, surprised both by the beauty of the young woman's nudity
and the violence of the scene.

The sculptor leans over the woman whose contours he is discovering in the light. He doesn't dare touch her.

He turns to Mesihi.

Suddenly he rushes at Mesihi, shouting; he punches him in
the face, half stunning him; instinctively, Mesihi lifts the dagger to protect himself and wounds Michelangelo in the arm;

insensitive to fear, the sculptor hits him again, catches hold of his wrist, and twists; he twists, he is strong; he is powerful and wounded and if Maringhi's servants hadn't intervened to overcome him, not only would Mesihi's bones have been broken, but, once Michelangelo had the dagger in his possession, he would surely have finished the poet off with a thousand furious blows.

MICHELANGELO IS TOO SURPRISED AND WEAKENED, too shocked to cry. He let his arm be bandaged by Manuel; the dagger opened up a good-sized, very straight wound on his biceps. One last time he secretly stroked the singer's hair, her body cold as marble; he avoided looking at her face, her closed eyes.

Then the corpse disappeared.

For a long time Michelangelo remained sitting on his bed, his heart pounding, trying to understand, and then he understood.

He understood Mesihi's terrible vengeance, his atrocious jealousy; he pictures the poet acting in cold blood, at night, and the thought makes him tremble.

He preferred to kill the young woman so she wouldn't snatch Michelangelo away from him.

The sculptor shivers with anger and pain.

It will take him months to be able to sleep again.

MESIHI DECIDED TO KEEP QUIET.

He fled into the night, also wounded, his wrist in pain; he smoked some opium, drank till he vomited, but nothing helped. He keeps seeing the image of that body standing in the half light, weapon in hand; he remembers having rushed toward her, he remembers struggling; she cried out, fought back; then she stopped fighting, when he had the knife; no matter how hard he tries to remember, he is incapable of understanding what happened after, how he felt the contact of a breast against his chest, the young woman sighing and giving way, then falling, wounded to death.

It seemed to him as if she threw herself onto the blade.

He will never know.

Mesihi is drunk without being drunk.

He trembles; cries in solitude; he wraps himself up in a dark woolen cloak, frail rampart against the world, when day breaks.

Buonarroto, I don't have time to answer your letter, since it's night; and even when I will have the time, I couldn't give you a firm answer, since I don't see the end of my business here. I'll be near you soon and then I'll do everything I can for you, as I have done up to now. I myself feel worse than ever, wounded and overcome with great fatigue; but I have the patience to try to reach my goal. So you can be patient for a little while, since you are 10,000 times more fortunate than I am right now.

Your Michelagnolo

MESIHI REMAINED SILENT.

He sacrificed his love one last time, hoping for nothing in return.

He defended the Frank against his enemy, saved him, that's what matters; too bad if by saving him he has lost him forever.

He will forget him, who knows, in the taverns of Tahtakale, in the arms of ephebes and singers with houris' eyes who will come massage his thighs; in the beauty of poetry and calligraphy.

He cries often; only the coming of night and debauchery brings him a little comfort.

FOUR WOOLEN SHIRTS, ONE OF THEM TORN AND bloodstained; two flannel doublets; one surcoat of the same material; three quills and the same number of inkpots; one broken mirror; four sheets of paper covered with drawings; two more covered with writing; three pairs of hose; one compass; some red chalk in a lead box; one silver case containing smelling salts; one cup of the same metal: that is the exact inventory of what is to be found in Michelangelo's room after his departure, methodically written down by Ottoman scribes.

He leaves Constantinople in secret. Pursued by the presence of death, overwhelmed by the memory of a love he was unable to give before it was too late, betrayed, he thinks, by Mesihi's jealousy, deceived by the powerful, urged by his brothers and the prospect of returning to the service of the Pope, he takes flight, just as he fled Rome three months earlier, wounded, torn apart, broken.

He leaves Istanbul without a penny.

Mesihi no longer presented himself at Maringhi's home.

Michelangelo wasn't sure about having him summoned, he couldn't make up his mind.

He organized his flight with Manuel; Michelangelo is unaware that, from afar, it's Arslan who made the arrangements, found the Venetian craft that will deposit him in Ancona, and paid most of the cost for the journey.

They are ridding themselves of the cumbersome artist lost between two shores.

On the night of his departure, on the quay at the foot of the ramparts, the divine Michelangelo is nothing but a wounded, frightened body, wrapped in a black kaftan, impatient for them to set sail, impatient to see Florence again.

A few hundred meters behind them, upstream, stands the black shape of the scaffolding for the buttress of the bridge that Michelangelo will not see.

He embraces Manuel for a long time, as if he were someone else, then climbs aboard. He feels a dull pain in his chest, which he attributes to his wound; tears spring to his eyes.

The only object he takes with him is his notebook, in which he jots down a few last words, as the ship is passing Seraglio Point.

Appear, show through, shine.
Sparkle, scintillate, go out.

HIDDEN BY THE BOATS, MESIHI QUICKLY TURNS AWAY.
He doesn't want to watch any longer, there's nothing more to
see: dark oars striking obscure waves, a square sail whose white-
ness doesn't manage to pierce the night.

He will go lose himself in the city streets, lose himself in the
hovels of Tahtakale; his sole souvenir of Michelangelo is the
drawing of an elephant, and especially, in a fold of his clothing,
the black-and-gold dagger that is burning into his belly now as
if it were white-hot.

EPILOGUE

On September 14, 1509, just as Michelangelo was starting work on the Sistine Chapel, a terrible earthquake struck Istanbul. Chroniclers describe the awful damage in detail: 109 mosques and 1,070 houses are completely destroyed; several thousand men, women, and children die, buried in the rubble. They write that in the house of the Vizier Mustafa Pasha alone 300 knights die along with their 300 horses. The ramparts collapse partially on the sea side, and completely on the land side; the hospice for the poor and a large part of the complex of Bayezid's mosque are destroyed. The plaster covering the Byzantine mosaics in Hagia Sophia cracks, revealing portraits of the Evangelists, which protect churches so well, say the Christians, that not a single church is damaged.

In any case the saints aren't concerned with Michelangelo's bridge, of which the piers, buttress, and the first few arches have already been erected: weakened, the work collapses; its rubble will be carried off to the Bosphorus by the water, stirred into fury by the earthquake, and no one will talk about it again.

TWO YEARS LATER, ON AUGUST 5, 1511, WHILE MI-chelangelo, his back bent, is still working on his scaffold in the Sistine Chapel, Ali Pasha passes away. The first great vizier to be killed in combat, he died on horseback, surrounded by his Janissaries, hit in the chest by an arrow from one of the Shi'ites from the East, the Tekke, whose rebellion he was trying to quell. They write that he would be avenged in a horrible way by Ismail, the new King of Persia, who wanted to reconcile with his powerful neighbor, after he had used the revolts to assert his power; captured, the killers of the Grand Vizier would be hurled into a pot of boiling water. They screamed a lot, it is said, before they were cooked and devoured by their guards.

This terrible vengeance would change nothing for Mesihi. The destitute poet, drunk and without a protector, killed himself even before the famous ceiling where God gives life to an Adam whose face so resembles that of the Turkish poet was finished.

Two extended fingers that don't touch each other.

Mesihi died at sunset on a July evening in 1512, poor and alone, after having sought a new patron in vain. We have one of his last verses:

My God, do not send me to the grave before
my body can caress my friend's chest.

Perhaps because he was a miscreant and a killer despite himself, or simply because his prayer was indecent, it will not be granted; he will die in a prosaic death rattle, a raucous breath soon swallowed up by the summons to sunset prayer, already streaming from countless minarets.

SULTAN BAYEZID, THE SECOND SULTAN TO BEAR THAT name, loved bridges.

Among the artworks he had built in the twenty-four Asian and thirty-four European provinces that then made up his empire, we can list: one nine-arch bridge over the Kizilirmak in Osmancik; a fourteen-arch bridge over the Sakarya; a nineteen-arch over the Hermos in Sarukhan; a six-arch over the Khabur, an eight-arch over the Valta in Armenia; one of eleven short, solid arches to let the army pass over it near Edirne; not to mention all the wooden bridges thrown haphazardly over the least consequential bodies of water that his janissaries or administrators encountered.

He died soon after abdicating in favor of his son Selim, in 1512, as he was on his way to Dimetoka, his birthplace. He never reached it: the poison administered by one of Selim's henchmen, or those other venoms known as sadness and melancholy, got the better of the sultan who had dreamed of a masterwork signed by Leonardo da Vinci or Michelangelo Buonarroti in Istanbul: he gave up his soul near the village of Aya, they say, beneath his red-and-gold dais, near the pier of a little bridge on the Adrianople road, in whose shadow he had been placed.

A LONG TIME AFTERWARD, IN FEBRUARY 1564, MI-chelangelo is preparing for his own death.

Seventeen large marble statues, hundreds of square meters of frescoes, a chapel, a church, a library, the dome of the most famous temple in the Catholic world, several palaces, one square in Rome, some fortifications in Florence, 300 poems, sonnets, and madrigals, just as many drawings and sketches, a name linked forever with Art, Beauty, and Genius: that, among other things, is what Michelangelo is getting ready to leave behind him, a few days before his eighty-ninth birthday, sixty years after his journey to Constantinople. He is dying wealthy, his dream realized: he has returned its past glory and possessions to his family. He hopes to see God, he will surely see Him, since he believes in Him.

It's a long time, sixty years.

In the meantime, he has written some love sonnets, despite not having experienced love, clinging to the memory of a lock of dead hair.

Often, he strokes the white scar on his arm and thinks about his lost friend Mesihi.

Of Istanbul, he remembers a vague light, a subtle sweetness mixed with bitterness, a distant music, soft shapes, pleasures rusted by time, the pain of violence, of loss: the abandon of hands that life did not let him touch, faces he'll never caress, bridges that haven't even yet been raised.

NOTE

The opening quotation about kings and elephants is from Kipling's introduction to *Life's Handicap*.

As for the story recounted in this novel, here is what we can retrace easily:

The Sultan's invitation is related by Ascanio Condivi (biographer and friend of Michelangelo), and is also mentioned by Giorgio Vasari. Leonardo da Vinci's drawing for a bridge over the Golden Horn does indeed exist, and is preserved at the Museum of Science in Milan.

Michelangelo's letters to his brother Buonarroto and to Sangallo quoted here are authentic; I have translated them from his *Carteggio*. The plans of Hagia Sophia sent to Sangallo by Michelangelo can be found in the Vatican Apostolic Library, in the Barberini Codex.

The sketch "Project for a Bridge for the Golden Horn" attributed to Michelangelo was recently discovered in the Ottoman archives, as well as the inventory of possessions abandoned in his room.

Dinocrates's anecdote appears in Vitruvius, at the beginning of Book II of *Elements of Architecture*.

The story about the sultan and the Andalusian vizier corresponds to an episode in the eventful biography of Al-Mu'tamid ibn Abbad, the last ruler of the taifa of Seville.

The black damask steel dagger inlaid with gold is exhibited in the treasure room at Topkapı Palace.

The biography of Mesihi of Prishtina the *shahrengiz* figures in all the histories of Ottoman literature, but mainly in Gibb, in the second volume, along with the extracts of his poetry reproduced here.

The lives of Bayezid the Second, his Vizier Ali Pasha, and the Genoese page Menavino (my Falachi) are largely documented in contemporary or subsequent chronicles.

The earthquake that hit Istanbul in 1509 is unfortunately real, as is the damage it did.

For the rest, we know nothing.